THE Missing Sunrise

Joan Oppenheimer

SCHOLASTIC INC.
New York Toronto London Auckland Sydney Tokyo

*For my grandchildren, whose
great-grandfather Luther Oppenheimer
is fictionalized in this story.*

Cover Photograph by Owen Brown

ISBN 0-590-32561-2

12 11 10 9 8 7 6 5 4 3 2 1   7   3 4 5 6 7/8

Printed in the U. S. A.   06

THE Missing Sunrise

A Windswept Book

WINDSWEPT TITLES
FROM SCHOLASTIC

1

I never thought I had any more ESP than the average person is supposed to have. But that day in August made me wonder if I'd been mistaken about my psychic abilities.

The moment I opened my eyes that morning, Gretchen von Weber emerged from a door in my mind that I'd firmly closed a couple years before. Couldn't stop thinking about her, no matter how I tried. Believe me, I did try, because it meant I thought about her brother Hunter, as well. There's absolutely no point in dwelling on ancient history when it's as frustrating as it is painful.

Mom came home for lunch that day, and she finally asked why I was so quiet. "You feel okay, Alexandra? You shouldn't have mowed the lawn, not in this heat."

I smiled at her. We've always had a good relationship, but it's been especially close since my father died last year. "I finished before it got hot. If I'm going to have a couple weeks vacation, it'll be nice to goof off at the beach or somewhere. I won't have to worry about the yard or —" I left it dangling. Her face had tightened, making it clear my light words weren't kidding anybody.

Neither of us was happy about the restaurant giving me two weeks off without pay. Not when my ancient car was in for repair, and I needed money more than a vacation. My college fund still looked pitifully inadequate. I'm seventeen, and there'll be another year to add to my bank account, but jobs are scarce in San Diego. I had to admit I was just as scared about the future as my mother.

Still, I couldn't stand to see the worry in her eyes. Without stopping to think, anxious to divert her, I blurted out the first thing that came to mind. "It's the craziest thing. Ever since I woke up this morning, I've been thinking about Gretchen von Weber."

Mom drew in her breath. "Oh, honey, I'm sorry. I might have known I'd forget if I didn't write it down. But it was so late — way past eleven — and I raced out to the kitchen before the phone rang again and woke you. Can't imagine why she called at that hour. She did apologize, said she hadn't realized it was so late."

"Who?" I said, totally confused.

"Why, Gretchen, of course. Gretchen von Weber. She said she'd call you back today."

"What on earth —?" I stared at her, my scalp

prickling with that uneasy speculation about ESP. Spooky, the way Gretchen came into my mind out of the blue, and now to hear she'd called last night. . . . "It's been two years," I said. "One letter and a couple of Christmas cards and — what did she want?"

Mom shrugged. "Didn't say." She glanced at her watch, swallowed the last of her iced tea, and got to her feet. "I'll be home around five. We need milk and butter. Anything else?"

I shook my head, only half-aware of her question.

She went through the kitchen, pausing only to check the shopping list on the refrigerator door. A very attractive lady, my mother. Medium height, nice figure, blond. Her hair a few shades darker than mine, and our eyes are identical, gray and wide-spaced. We wear the same size in everything but shoes.

I sat at the table for a long time after her car went down the drive. Even while I washed our dishes, together with the breakfast things that I'd skipped to get the yard done while it was cool, I worked automatically. My thoughts had returned to a day four years before, when one of my friends came over with startling news.

Tammy flopped across the other bed as I sat on mine, legs folded, facing her. "You'll never guess!" she said and rattled on without giving me a chance. "Gretchen von Weber's coming to visit for two whole weeks. Then I'm going home with her for a while. And you know what I was thinking? Maybe we could work it so you can go, too. Wouldn't that be neat?"

"Where does she live?"

Tammy looked at me, startled. "Gretchen von Weber," she said patiently. "You know. The big ranch up in the Laguna Mountains. Meadowmount." She saw my blank look. "Thought I told you about her. Well, even if I didn't, you must have heard about the von Webers. Her great-grandfather Luther and his fabulous necklace? The Alaskan Sunrise?"

"The Alaskan who?" At thirteen, my reading was limited to mysteries, biographies of interesting people like Amelia Earhart, and the stuff I had to read for book reports.

Tammy sighed. "Okay, I'll take it from the top. Gretchen's our age, and she lives with her father, who's a turkey, and her stepmother, ditto, and her great-grandfather, who's over ninety years old and absolutely fantastic."

"He's—is he really that old?"

She nodded. "And bright and cute and funny — Grandpa's terrific. You'll love him." She rolled over on her back and addressed the ceiling, left ankle balanced on her right knee. "When he was only sixteen, he came across the country in a covered wagon from — oh, someplace in Iowa. All by himself, nothing in his pocket but a twenty-dollar gold piece. Just like the pioneers, for Pete's sake. He says he planted a crop of wheat and sold it to buy passage on the *City of Seattle*." She turned her head to grin at me. "Where do you think he wanted to go? I'll give you a clue. The year was 1898."

She had my attention by that time. "Alaska? The gold fields?"

"Correct. You've just won a barrel of popcorn. Want to try for a year's supply of jelly beans?"

I ignored that. "So did he find any gold? Wow, only sixteen and crossing the country all by himself. There must have been Indians then and — what a *trip* —"

Tammy went on talking to the ceiling. "So then, on his way up there on the boat, he teamed up with somebody a little older. Herman Braun was twenty-two, a German immigrant. And a year later, the two of them took a humungous amount of gold home with them. Their families are still really close, even though Herman settled in San Francisco, and Grandpa came down here to San Diego. He built Meadowmount when he married his wife Caroline. Grandpa just worshipped her. The Sunrise — the necklace I told you about — that was his wedding present to her."

"What's it like?" I asked, curious. "All diamonds?"

Her head moved from side to side. "Mostly gold. His partner started a — what do you call it? — import business. And he had the necklace made by Chinese artisans. You'll see it for yourself if you can come to Meadowmount with Gretchen and me. It has a diamond clasp, but the necklace itself is a string of carved golden animals, all kinds. Their eyes are rubies and emeralds and — haven't you ever read about it? My dad says it's famous all over the world."

Even then I was captivated by the idea that Luther von Weber had given this magnificent gift to the bride he adored. Later, when I realized the Sunrise was indeed famed as a priceless art object, I still found its romantic history far more intriguing.

"You've got to persuade your parents that it's okay to go back with Gretchen and me. It means a lot to her to have friends come and visit. How would you like living in a place with electrified walls all around it and guard dogs and —"

"You're putting me on." I laughed, then saw by her expression that she was serious. "Walls and dogs? Sounds like the state prison."

Tammy said, "Mmmhmm. Well, Dad says the insurance companies aren't wild about the Sunrise staying on private property, even with all that protection. You know. I think Gretchen's going away to school this fall. Hunter, too. That's her brother. Oh, wow. Wait'll you meet Hunter." She rolled her eyes, clearly a positive response.

As it turned out, I had an identical reaction a few weeks later. But first I met Gretchen and liked her immediately. She was petite, but put together in perfect proportion, not all bust and bottom like a lot of small girls. Big brown eyes dominated a lively face framed by thick dark hair and a slant of bangs.

While Tammy introduced us, Gretchen stared

at me. "Your hair's fantastic," she said in a soft, breathless voice. "What do you call it? Silver-blond? And along with everything else, a name like Alexandra."

Usually, when people come on that strong, I put up my guard immediately. But I could tell Gretchen wasn't a phony. That first day, I sized her up as impulsive, generous, and possibly a little immature. Not too surprising, of course, for somebody raised in a place like Meadowmount, as another possession to be guarded. *She must hate that,* I thought.

My first stay at Meadowmount confirmed that suspicion. The enormous two-story house with the gabled roof had been built in the thirties. It had a glorious setting — mountains behind it, a lake and a slope of green and golden meadow in front.

During frequent visits, Gretchen and I formed a friendship that endured long after Tammy moved to the East Coast. I developed a unique feeling for Meadowmount, too, one compounded of respect and awe. If Gretchen didn't much resemble a garden variety of enchanted princess, her home certainly looked like a fairy-tale abode. There was a silver cast to the weathered gray wood of the big house, its shutters a darker shade. The place had a secretive look, as if the house had gathered in upon itself in silent meditation, waiting for some mystic spell to be broken.

In those blithe years from thirteen to fifteen, I figured a coat of paint in a lighter color might accomplish that. Later, I knew it wouldn't be that simple. By that time, the same spell had captured me, and I gave my heart, rashly and entirely without his knowledge, to Gretchen's brother.

Hunter's dark eyes seemed entirely black, though I knew that to be biologically impossible. His features were strong, a straight nose and firm mouth that rarely smiled, even when amusement softened those brooding eyes. He was not extraordinarily good-looking, but he had the indefinable quality my drama teacher would call "presence." People always looked twice at him. Like him or not, they never overlooked Hunter von Weber.

He overlooked *me*, however, entirely indifferent toward his kid sister's frequent houseguest. Shortly after my fifteenth birthday, with our household in turmoil during my father's terminal illness, I began to decline Gretchen's invitations. That was partly because I could no longer return her hospitality, but I think she knew the real reason. I simply found it too painful to be around Hunter, feeling as I did about him.

She wrote me a lovely, warm letter after my father died. Gretchen always had the knack of saying the right thing in precisely the right way. Maybe because she truly cared about people and believed in letting them know it.

"I miss you, Alex," she said at the end of that letter. "You'll always be a special friend, even if we don't see each other again. And I hope we will. You're one of those people who could call and say, 'I need you, Gretchen,' and I'd come running. Remember that. Please, Alex, if it would help to talk, do call. I'll come there or meet you somewhere else, if you don't want to come to Meadowmount."

I think she understood even then that I never wanted to see Meadowmount or her brother again. I'm ashamed to say that I answered her wonderful letter with only a scrawled line on the bottom of a printed thank-you card. It had been over a year since she wrote those warm words of sympathy.

The phone rang as I hung up the dishcloth, the sound jolting me rudely back to the present. I hesitated, letting it ring again. Gretchen? What did she want? After all this time, why would she call me?

She sounded exactly the same, and the low, breathless words swept away the years since I last heard her voice. "Oh, Alex, it's great to talk to you. I can't believe it's been so long. And please tell your mother again how sorry I am about calling last night. Couldn't believe it was that late. Dumb thing to do."

"No problem," I said. "Mom's still a night owl, especially since —"

Gretchen picked up on the words I hadn't said — "since Dad died"— just as she always did. "How are you two getting along? Is your mom working? The phone number hasn't been changed. Are you living in the same place?"

I explained briefly that we'd sold the house and were in a small duplex nearby. "Better for just the two of us." Cheaper, too. I told her where Mom was working and mentioned my part-time job and the weeks I'd have off. A moment later, I regretted that lapse.

"Then you'll be free next week! Listen, Alex, I'm having an old-fashioned house party, and I especially want *you*. Peter Braun is here. Remember how I always said I'd marry him, so our two families would be merged forever? You know, it just might happen." She laughed.

"Gretchen, I'm not sure —"

"— and Corey Atkinson, the guy who lives down the road. He always used to be in and out of the house when you came to visit. You know him, too. And Bonnie Layton's stalking Hunter these days — the pun is intentional. So if you're free that week, it'll be just perfect."

"I don't know, Gretchen," I said uncomfortably. "It's — oh, my car's in the garage, for one thing. And even if I get it back in time, I wouldn't trust it on mountain roads. I don't trust it twenty miles in any direction, so —"

"Alex."

I stopped. Abruptly, in the way she said my name, she didn't sound like the old happy, bubbling Gretchen anymore. I couldn't analyze it right then because she went on after a moment.

"Alex, remember the letter I wrote you after your father died?"

"Yes."

"I said you were — a special friend. Remember?"

"Yes." I swallowed hard. "I read that letter so many times, I can practically recite it by heart."

"Then I hope you'll stop giving me excuses about the party, when we both know I wouldn't ask you if I — if I didn't need you. I mean that, Alex." She said again quietly, "I need you."

I bit my lip. "Then I'll come to the house party, of course. Have to check with Mom first, but —"

I heard a sigh on the line. "Great. I'll have Hunter pick you up. Friday, about four. That'll give you three whole days to get ready. We can talk when you get here. Oh, it'll help so much to be able to talk to you, Alex."

"Gretchen," I said impulsively, "is Grandpa — ?"

"He's fine." I heard the smile in her voice. "Just the same as always. He'll be so pleased when I tell him you're coming."

We said good-bye, and I stood for several moments staring at the phone. Gretchen might have been prone to melodramatic behavior at the age of thirteen, but she'd certainly outgrown the tendency by now. Even so, I might have discounted the tension in her voice as a possible overreaction to some minor problem, except for one thing.

After she hung up, I heard a second distinct and unmistakable click on the line. Someone at Meadowmount had been listening.

Two days later, I received an anonymous note in the mail, just a couple of lines printed on a piece of lined tablet paper. *If Gretchen invites you to Meadowmount, don't go! There's someone there who doesn't want you around.*

After the initial shock and anger, I felt a little chill creeping up my neck. Whoever had written those words didn't know me very well. Otherwise, they'd realize a cryptic warning like that would only arouse my stubborn streak, even if it hurt my pride at the same time.

Besides, the crudely printed message reinforced Gretchen's plea. She must need somebody she could trust. But why couldn't she talk to Grandpa? Or Hunter? Or Peter? Or even Margaret Langhorst? The housekeeper had always doted on Gretchen. What was going on at Meadowmount, anyway? Why had Gretchen reached outside the household and her circle of friends to call on someone she hadn't seen in two years?

In the past couple of days, I'd wavered once or twice, tempted to cancel out on the invitation. Predictably, my mother had been delighted about it. "You'll have some fun for a change," she insisted. "You've been working entirely too hard."

As it turned out, I fully accepted the decision to go to Meadowmount in the moments before I drifted off to sleep that night. Gretchen's words echoed in my mind. When I finally defined the odd strain in her voice, it jolted me awake again.

It was desperation I had heard when she said quietly, "I need you, Alex."

By two o'clock on Friday afternoon, I had packed my bag, showered, and dressed. I'd changed my mind and my outfit three times, looking for a smashing effect that would make Hunter notice instantly that Alex Hammond had grown up. At last, furious with myself for falling back into the same futile, make-him-notice-me routine, I settled for a sleeveless pink blouse and a white pleated skirt. It would be hotter than the hinges of Satan's domain in the mountains.

For a couple of hours, in between last-minute reminders in a note to my mother about things like watering the plants, I paced and dithered. Luckily, Hunter arrived fifteen minutes early, a matter of seconds before I fell apart.

When his car came up the drive, my heart began to hammer against my ribs, and I whispered fiercely, "Stop it! Just stop that right now!" It didn't slow down, of course, any more than it had years ago, automatically beating faster whenever I found myself in the same room with Hunter.

As he got out of the car, I saw he was taller at eighteen, his chest and shoulders broader. Something about his face seemed different, too, in a subtle way less boyish.

I opened the door, and he stepped into the entry hall, looking at me silently, his dark glasses hiding his eyes. "Hi, Alex. You're growing up, aren't you?"

"I guess so." But not enough so I could come up with a better line than that one. I saw the small beads of perspiration on his upper lip. "Thirsty? There's lemonade and iced tea in the fridge."

"Lemonade? Great."

In the kitchen, he drank half the contents of a tall glass, then leaned against the counter, studying me. "There's something I have to tell you, Alex. I wanted to explain in person, not on the phone. I think it'd be wise to call off this house party Gretchen's so set on."

I stared at him, wondering for one wild moment if Hunter might be the person who had sent the anonymous note suggesting that I stay away from Meadowmount. Then I realized he'd never stoop to anything so sneaky. When he had something to say, he spit it out, regardless of consequences. As he was about to do now.

"Why?" I said at last. "What's happened?"

His face went still for a moment and the hand lifting the glass to his mouth paused in midair. Then he drank the last of the lemonade and put the glass on the counter. "Gretch had a — a kind of accident this morning. Fell down the stairs. She's — there's a possibility of concussion, sprained her ankle and —"

"Oh, the poor thing!" I pictured the sweeping flight of stairs at Meadowmount. It must have been a nasty fall. "How in the world did it happen?"

Hunter shook his head, brushed his hair back from his forehead. "Peter hasn't given me any details. Except that" — he scowled abruptly — "Gretchen won't hear of scrubbing the party plans, even if she's laid up for a couple days. She's set on you coming, especially. Not next week. Now. Today."

I watched him, but I didn't say anything. In my mind, a cold, ugly question slowly took shape. Clearly, something was going on at Meadowmount. Gretchen had begged me to come because she needed me. Then she fell down that long flight of stairs. Gretchen, the most graceful person I've ever known, a natural athlete.

Had it really been an accident?

2 ━━━

For the most part, the long drive was a silent one and uncomfortable as well, at least for me. We hit the late afternoon traffic, and Hunter struggled with that for the first half hour, leaving me to my thoughts.

He wasn't happy with me, since I'd ignored his hints that it be better if I stayed home. Not only that, I'd evaded giving him a definite promise that I'd leave after a short visit with Gretchen.

"Let me play it by ear," I said, "after I talk to her. Okay?"

"Listen, Alex, there's something you don't understand. Even I don't know exactly what's going on at Meadowmount, but the vibes are *bad*."

"Yes."

He turned to glance at me. "How much did Gretch tell you?"

"Only enough so I picked up on — something wrong."

I decided not to mention the fact that someone had listened in on that conversation, or about the anonymous note. By that time I felt unhappy with him, too, for maneuvering me into an awkward, embarrassing situation. Perversely, I directed my general irritation at him, though it consisted in part of a vague guilt. I hadn't told my mother about the letter, either, or about the person who'd eavesdropped on Gretchen's phone call.

I hadn't wanted to accept the invitation to the house party in the first place. But once I decided to go, convinced she really did need me, the only person she could trust for some mysterious reason, I had no intention of backing away from the situation. At least not until I'd talked to her.

So I sat beside Hunter, rigid with tension, far too aware of him, my chin up, face burning with the emotions churning inside me. Questions, too. Who had sent me that note? Certainly not Grandpa or Gretchen's parents, Kendall and Delphine. Or the housekeeper and her husband, Margaret and Alden Langhorst. Or the caretaker and general manager, Niles Benson. It was a childish, spiteful thing, sending someone an anonymous letter. The adults at Meadowmount surely wouldn't have been involved in something like that.

Yet it seemed to me that the kids wouldn't do anything so underhanded, either. Peter Braun or

Corey Atkinson? Why would they care whether or not I was included on the guest list? Gretchen had invited me, and Hunter had never looked at me twice. If he felt strongly that the party should be canceled — and clearly he did — he had already handled it in the way Hunter handled everything — openly, directly, and bluntly.

That left only one person who might be responsible. Bonnie Layton. And I couldn't imagine why she'd care one way or another whether I appeared at Meadowmount. I remembered Bonnie as a terrifically attractive girl with beautiful chestnut hair, too involved with her own gorgeous self to think twice about anyone else. Years ago, I'd tried to be nice to her for Gretchen's sake, but that didn't mean I ever learned to like her.

Eventually, Hunter roused himself to comment as he nodded at the sloping hillside by the freeway. "Remember our heavy spring rains? Hills were all green, and along here the banks were one mass of color with the wild flowers. Grass is already brown," he added unnecessarily and on a mild note of reproach. "You should have come up earlier in the season."

I forced a smile. "I'm sorry I missed the yuccas in bloom." My spirits lifted as I recalled seeing them years before. Yuccas aren't too common outside the desert or mountain areas where they thrive, bizarre and quite lovely with floral spikes that can reach a height of five or six feet. Their clustered blossoms range in color from golden green to brilliant butter-yellow.

Hunter squinted out the side window for a moment. "Lots of brush now. Look at the heavy undergrowth." He added wryly, "Guess we always have something to complain about. Most years, it's because we get too little rain. Now we've had a good amount, and they're still worried about fire danger." He shrugged. "We're due, I suppose."

I recalled a fire station run by the forest service several miles down the highway from the road that cut off onto von Weber land. The area was picturesque, with a tract of summer homes, most of them A-frames, a small redwood church and a redwood school, and a few cabins mingling with luxurious lodges scattered deep in the trees.

Watching for familiar landmarks, I felt eagerness stir within at the prospect of seeing Gretchen and Meadowmount again. We entered foothills pocked with blue granite boulders. The huge oaks gave way to pines as the road wound upward, and the air freshened with their fragrance.

This was a new macadam road covered with pulverized rock to prevent a slippery surface in snow season. We passed an occasional field with Black Angus cattle or white-faced Herefords, and a ranch that raised Charolais, an experimental breed of white, blocky animals.

Higher, I noted a slope with the twisted, blackened skeletons of squat oaks which had not survived the last fire in the area. Curiously, most of the pine trees had. Though the bark on their trunks was black, they flourished, their boughs green and full of life.

At last came the stretch of high meadows, wooded slopes receding, and a lake, placid in the silver haze of twilight. Already, ducks huddled on one bank, settling for the night.

The little car slowed and swung onto a blacktop road. I had a glimpse of a swinging sign as we passed and recalled the first time I saw it and teased Gretchen about its brevity.

"Only your name, von Weber? Why doesn't it say Meadowmount? Or a ranch name, like all the other places around here?"

She laughed. "You mean something really hilarious like Back Acres? But you know, I did ask Grandpa about another sign once, and he just said, 'Ours is adequate.' Grandma Caroline was the one who named Meadowmount, and even she couldn't get him to put it on the sign."

As we rounded a curve, I drew in my breath. The familiar gray walls loomed ahead. Beyond, on higher ground, stood Meadowmount, windows blazing with the reflection of the setting sun.

As we approached the massive gate, Hunter honked, and it swung open. Niles Benson stood in the door of the cottage, arms folded across his chest as he watched us pass. Looking through the rear window, I saw him reach inside and knew he pressed a button on a wall panel there. Slowly, the gate closed.

Niles was a silent, rather stern individual who spent little time in the big house, I recalled, appearing only for meals, as a rule. A loner, he preferred to live in the gatehouse with the current guard dogs, a cross between Norwegian elkhound and German shepherd, which he had raised and trained himself.

"Does he have the same dogs?" I asked Hunter. It was only a way of pretending a casual interest in something other than my return to this place, and my mixed feelings about that. Those emotions included a keen regret that I hadn't grown out of my foolish crush on Hunter.

"Sure," he said. "Soldier and Lingo are still around. It'll be interesting to see if they remember you. Niles swears they never forget anyone who's stayed here for any length of time."

He paused, then added, "But don't gamble on that. I wouldn't go outside tonight if I were you, until Niles takes you out first to test the dogs' memories."

He parked in the graveled area a short distance from the front door, turned off the motor, and in the silence that followed, stared at me.

For a moment, I felt uneasily aware of his gaze. Then I looked past him at the house, relieved to see it was exactly as I remembered. Meadowmount was not beautiful. It lacked grace and proportion, two wings tacked on almost in afterthought from the original square structure. Several chimneys interrupted the lines of the gable roof. I recalled my fascination at thirteen with a place that boasted six fireplaces.

Somehow, the house had mellowed over the years, through storms it had weathered and under the onslaught of the hot, bright summer sun. It stood, solid and dignified and proud, as little changed as the enormous ancient oaks on the hillside in the distance.

Margaret, the housekeeper, met us at the door. Her round face was distraught, and her eyes looked swollen as if she'd been crying. As she called to her husband, I heard a hint of temper in her voice.

"Alden? Alden! Come help get these bags upstairs." She added to me, crossly, "The man's like fog, the way he comes and goes, never making any noise about it."

Then, plump little hands on my shoulders, she looked at me, her slightly protruding eyes close to mine. "Well, here you are again, Alexandra, almost all grown-up. And as beautiful as we all said you'd be one day."

"Thank you, Mrs. Langhorst. It's nice to see you — and Meadowmount. I'm glad nothing's changed."

Her face tightened. She shook her head. "I only wish that were so," she said.

"How's Gretchen?"

"Still in a good bit of pain, I'm sorry to say. I hope she's sleeping by now." She hesitated. "I've put you in the same room you used to have, right next to her. But it might be best to wait till morning to see her."

I turned to note that Hunter had disappeared. Alden Langhorst came into the entry hall to get the bags, nodding gravely at me, and I followed him up the wide stairs. Lights winked on as we went, and I smiled at Margaret standing by the switch below, guessing what was in her mind. One accident on these steps was enough.

22

How on earth could Gretchen have tripped? She'd lived in this house all her life. People did fall downstairs, of course, but rarely anyone as surefooted or with as much natural coordination as Gretchen.

Alden mumbled something as he deposited the bags in my room, then went unhurriedly back to the hall. A stocky man with a barrel chest and an unremarkable face, he was as much a part of the background at Meadowmount as one of the massive antiques that his wife regularly polished with lemon oil.

I recalled Gretchen telling me that as teenagers in World War II, they escaped from East Berlin just ahead of the Russians. They met in some sort of refugee camp, and in a year or two came with a group to this country. Eventually, the von Webers sponsored several members of that group, offering them employment at Meadowmount. Margaret and Alden had married and remained here.

It was difficult to imagine the strong-minded, plain-speaking Margaret as a girl my age, suffering unimaginable hardships in her native country. Her hulking, obedient husband remained a shadowy personality even now. If Alden ever rebelled against his wife's rule, it was probably with the occasional vanishing act Margaret complained about.

Dismissing them from my mind, I unpacked and took a quick shower. Refreshed, I came back to inspect the familiar room. It still looked pretty and feminine, though the drapes and spread and armchair were now done in lavender instead of blue.

On the chest of drawers stood a white vase with three massive Peace roses, each pale petal edged in pink. Their perfume drifted through the still, warm air, part of a serene, relaxing atmosphere that somehow failed to ease the tension within me.

I found myself listening, alert for the slightest sound from the door on the other side of the bath that separated my room from Gretchen's. At last, noting the shadows deepening, I dressed in a white blouse embroidered with golden flowers and my pleated skirt. Bonnie had probably arrived with bags full of fantastic designer outfits — her father was enormously wealthy — but I hadn't come up here to compete with the local clotheshorse. This summer, silk blouses and skirts were the only dressy items in my wardrobe.

Downstairs, I found Gretchen's father and stepmother in the huge room off the entry hall. Kendall came toward me with his slight smile, hand outstretched. His dark hair had pronounced streaks of gray at his temples and sideburns. I suspected he had aided nature the least bit, but it was very effective.

"Alexandra? It's good to see you again."

I realized with a faint amusement that I could never recall Kendall looking directly at me before, or addressing a comment to me. Gretchen's crowd, always around when she was home, had been asked to call her parents by their first names. I doubted whether they saw any of us as individuals, however, but rather as "one of the young people," as Kendall would probably put it.

"It's nice to be here." I smiled at him. "But I'm sorry about Gretchen's fall. How did it happen?"

He looked at me sharply. Then he lifted his shoulders in a gesture that indicated, along with his pained expression, that he found my direct question unfortunate.

"She fell," he said vaguely. "Always dark in that upstairs hall. Would you like a soft drink? Ginger ale, perhaps, or Seven-Up?"

"Oh, either would be fine, thank you." As he went to the small corner bar, I glanced around the high-beamed room furnished in the style Grandpa had told me was popular in the early part of the century. The dark, hand-carved Spanish furniture was covered with jewel-toned velvets and brocades. In the center of one wall was a fieldstone fireplace that Luther von Weber had built himself.

I walked past it to the far end of the room to speak to Gretchen's stepmother. She stood, half-turned from me, by the huge glass cabinet which contained her collection of crystal animals and figurines.

This fascination with fragile miniatures had always struck me as odd in someone like Delphine, a big, athletic woman with impressive shoulders. She looked like a retired P.E. teacher, and I knew she played better-than-average tennis and golf.

Delphine never made any secret of the fact that

she didn't much care about young people. She wasn't exactly rude, but merely indifferent, I recalled, not easy to talk to.

Gretchen and Hunter used to quote her malaprops with wicked glee, imitating Delphine's firm, no-nonsense tone. She loved Hawaii because of all the "erotic" plants and flowers. A minor squabble had been described as "a tempest in a teacup." More than once, we'd disgraced ourselves at the dinner table, breaking up over one of her better bobbles.

"Hello, Delphine. You're looking great. That green dress is wonderful with your hair."

She really did look great, her hair still the red-brown of an autumn leaf, her large eyes a clear, brilliant blue. At a distance, she seemed a dozen years younger than the age I suspected she must be.

Smiling tentatively, she glanced at her husband across the room, then back at me with a wider smile. It was a curiously childlike gesture, as if she'd asked and received his permission to respond to my compliment.

"Alexandra! Hunter said he'd brought you. We've been in a state of confusion, to say the least, since Gretchen took her tumble. Just before lunch, that was. Luckily, Corey was here. We could never get a doctor to come way out here, but Corey knew enough first aid to take charge after he checked with our Dr. Neeley on the phone. You remember him? No, not the doctor. I mean Corey."

It would be all but impossible to forget anybody like that, I thought, big, blond Corey with his year-round tan, a sensational contrast to light gray eyes and fair hair. It had come as a nice surprise to discover that he wasn't conceited, either, but bright and witty, a really nice guy. Peter Braun in his completely honest moments would admit that. But Hunter never had.

Kendall touched my elbow and gave me my soft drink, ice tinkling against the glass. "Did Hunter tell you that Peter and his father are visiting?"

I noted Delphine's quick, sidelong glance. There had been occasions in the past, I recalled, when I caught the big redheaded woman off guard and saw a keen intelligence in those expressive eyes. For reasons of her own, she seldom displayed any signs of a sharp intellect. I wondered at that once more, briefly. The conditioning of her generation? When she was a girl, it wouldn't have been considered smart to reveal a high I.Q. I was glad things had changed.

"I knew Peter was here," I said. "I didn't know his father had come, too."

She nodded. "He'll be having dinner upstairs. Grandpa doesn't always come down. He's not up to a lot of people these days."

My back to the door, I was not aware that Hunter had come in until I heard his voice.

"Grandpa loves having people around," he said crisply. "He doesn't come down because it hurts his pride when Alden has to carry him." He looked at Delphine and the air seemed to crackle between them. "On my way to get Alex,

I dropped off Grandpa's check. He's ordered the chair elevator."

The note of defiance in his voice hinted at a previous argument over the chair elevator, whatever that might be.

Hunter must have seen my puzzled expression, because he explained, "It's a chair that's attached to the stair banister, runs by electricity. With that, Grandpa can go up and down a dozen times a day if he wants to." His eyes were dark, opaque. "And no one will have to carry him."

"That was thoughtful of you, Hunter, to order it for him." Delphine's voice sounded smooth, but a bit high-pitched. "My only reservation, as you know, was possible harm to those magnificent old banisters. But if Grandpa feels this is something that will make him more comfortable, then of course —" She bowed her head slightly. "Meadowmount is his, after all."

I saw Kendall's hand tighten on her shoulder. "My dear, would you check on dinner, please? If it's going to be longer than another half hour, perhaps we could have a few tidbits in the meantime?"

They moved toward the hall. A moment later, I heard laughing voices outside the French doors behind us, and Bonnie and Corey came in from the terrace.

Bonnie looked incredibly beautiful, the glorious burnished hair now in a shorter, layered cut. She wore a beige dress with a halter top that showed off her glowing tan. When she saw me, she hesitated, green eyes slightly narrowed.

It was Corey who came toward me with a wide smile, so full of energy and vitality it radiated about him like an invisible aura. Never a restful person, he seemed to stimulate people around him, either to crazy conversation or frantic fun.

I held out my hand, but he used it only to draw me toward him. His lips were warm against my cheek. Then he grinned, his eyes shining with mischief. "You're even prettier than before, Alex. Is it something in the water down in San Diego?"

I felt my face burn. "Hi, Corey. You haven't changed a bit. Bonnie, good to see you again." *Lies,* I thought crossly. Both comments were totally untrue.

Bonnie gave me a silken smile that matched her voice. "I'd like to think you really are happy to see me," she said.

Confident her words had grabbed everyone's attention, she added softly, "Because somebody sent me a letter that said I shouldn't come to Meadowmount. I got it the day before I left home. And you know what? Whoever wrote it, why, they forgot to sign it —"

3

Clearly, Bonnie didn't believe me when I denied sending the letter. Her skeptical smile didn't fade, even when I told her I'd received one, too.

"But of course you never thought to bring it with you," she said, her tone sweet, ready to forgive me for a natural mistake.

"As a matter of fact, I did bring it along." In the echo of the sharp words, I took a deep breath. Too late, I recalled how Bonnie always used to bring out the worst in me. It had irritated me beyond endurance when I seemed to be the only one to pick up on her sugary zingers. I felt the heat of rising anger now as I glanced at Hunter, who was carefully deadpan, gazing out at the darkening garden.

Corey merely watched me with mild interest,

as if he realized I had almost blurted out the reason I'd brought the letter. But this was neither the time or place to go into my misgivings about Gretchen, nor were these three the proper people to confide in.

The dinner chime sounded. Corey must have heard my soft sigh of relief. He put his arm across my shoulders and bent to murmur, "Saved by the bell."

I glanced at him, wondering if he were more perceptive than I'd suspected. He merely raised thick blond brows, looking amused. And, except for modern clothing, every inch a Viking.

When we came into the hall, I saw Peter coming down the stairs and hurried to greet him. He wasn't as tall as Hunter and Corey, nor as good-looking, but I'd always liked the strength in his broad, blunt face.

He grinned. "Alex! You're lookin' great. Homely as ever." Head to one side, he studied me. Now that he was serious again, I saw a hardness in his eyes that I couldn't remember ever being there before.

"Gretch sends her love," he said. "She was really upset until Margaret came to tell her you'd arrived. Said you insisted on waiting till morning to see her. That was really thoughtful, Alex, and probably wise."

It was not precisely the way it had happened, but I let it pass. Margaret adored Gretchen, mothering her like the child she'd never had. I liked the idea of people protecting Gretchen right now, since I was unable to shake the strong feeling that she might have need of that protection.

Delphine put me between Peter and Hunter at the table. As usual, Hunter ignored me during the meal. Stung by his customary lack of interest, I concentrated on Peter, catching up on our lives and Gretchen's in the two years since we'd seen each other.

I sensed a tension and anger he could barely control when he spoke to anyone else at the table. He ate very little, pushing the food around on his plate, putting his fork down at last to give me his whole attention.

"My father's here with me this trip," he said in his low, warm voice.

"Yes, Delphine mentioned that. Any — any special reason he came along?" I asked the question partly because I saw he was bursting with something he wanted to tell me.

"I guess so." He gave me a wry smile. "It's still classified," he said. "My father doesn't believe in cluttering up my mind with details about things that don't concern me directly."

From what I knew about his rather strict German family, that didn't surprise me. I suspected, however, that Peter could make an educated guess about most of the things his father chose to treat as classified information. It seemed to mean that the reason behind Mr. Braun's trip to consult with his grandfather's old Alaskan partner was not the cause of Peter's poorly concealed rage. Nor did it have to do with whatever it was he wanted to share with me.

I saw him glance at the kitchen door, just swinging shut. Both Margaret and Alden had been waiting on the table. I tried to remember which one had just left the dining room, but could not. I had been too intent on the cold fury in Peter's dark eyes. A muscle jerked at the angle of his jaw. My own nerves tightening in response, I waited for him to speak.

He asked abruptly, "What do you know about Margaret's background?"

I stared at him, wondering what the connection might be between his father and the von Weber housekeeper. Then I realized he had deliberately changed the subject, perhaps aware that he had communicated his own unease.

"Not much," I said. "Only that she and Alden escaped from East Berlin when they were teenagers, just ahead of the Russian army."

At the other end of the table, Delphine and Bonnie were eagerly exchanging their impressions of a roadshow company of a Broadway musical. Under cover of that discussion, Peter spoke in a quiet, even voice.

"Margaret had a twin sister. Marlene stayed behind with the aunt and uncle who raised them. In the two years Margaret spent in a refugee camp in West Germany, she never received any word from the family she'd left. And never in the years since, either. She thought Marlene was dead. Until recently."

A chill went through me, prickling the hair on the back of my neck.

Peter scowled at the spoon he moved around on the snowy cloth. "It still isn't clear how the message got through. But the gist of it is, in return for a considerable amount of money, a certain person will bring the sister out of East Berlin. Marlene's husband, too, and a couple of grown children."

I drew in a ragged breath. I had read about several hair-raising escapes from behind the Berlin wall. "Poor Margaret. A twin — and children Margaret's never even seen. She'd want to gamble on saving them, but — couldn't it be a fraud?"

I remembered reading about things like that, too, clever con games victimizing the relatives of people behind the iron curtain. No wonder Margaret looked as if she'd been crying. And on top of that dilemma, she'd been terribly upset about Gretchen's fall.

Peter picked up the small spoon and sat for a moment, twisting it through his long fingers. "You get the picture," he said. "There's a name for people who help in escapes like that, *fluchthelfers*. Flight helpers. And of course a lot of them are legitimate. But some are crooks, and that's the problem here. Margaret's contact can't or won't show any proof that Marlene's still alive. And obviously he can't guarantee delivery. So you can imagine the position Grandpa's in —"

I shook my head to indicate he'd lost me.

"Margaret asked him for a loan," Peter said. "Put the whole thing on *his* shoulders." He gestured, and the spoon slid out of his fingers. He caught it deftly before it hit the table.

Delphine's voice cut through the low buzz of conversation to suggest we adjourn to the living room.

Peter drew my chair back, then bent forward to say softly, "There's something else —"

"Miss Hammond?"

I turned to see Niles, the caretaker, in the hall. "Hi, Mr. Benson. Would you like me to go out and see if Soldier and Lingo still remember me?"

He nodded. His thin face lit up as it always did at mention of his dogs. "You remembered their names," he said, pleased.

Peter touched my arm. "I'll come along, too, if you don't mind."

We followed Niles's slight figure to the front door. Outside, the moon had appeared over the mountains to the east. Below us, well beyond the wall, I could see its pale reflection on the dark waters of the lake. The sharp, eerie bark of a fox cut across the silence.

"It's so quiet," I said, my own voice hushed. "That's one thing I always forget about Meadowmount, that wonderful, peaceful quiet."

Peter made a low sound and gestured with one hand. "Out there, you'd find more death and violence than you can possibly imagine. Not very peaceful with all the predators on the prowl — coyotes, owls —" He turned to the caretaker. "Hunter said you shot a big cat last week over in the south meadow."

Niles corrected him with his usual precision about detail. "The rocks beyond the meadow. Dogs cornered it. Now we're on the lookout for its mate." He whistled.

Seconds later, Soldier and Lingo bounded around the side of the house, silvery coats glistening as they crossed the path of light from the big front windows. They slowed, catching my scent. Then, obeying Niles's soft command, they went to him and sat back on their haunches, tongues lolling, watching me warily.

I had a great deal of confidence in Niles as a dog trainer and in the dogs' respect for him. But I have to admit, when he beckoned me to come to them, the skin crawled on the back of my neck.

Soldier extended his muzzle to sniff my hand, then lay down, nose on his outstretched paws, looking almost comically indifferent. Lingo repeated the procedure, then looked up at me amiably as if to say, "Is that what you want?" After a few seconds, he took a step toward me and nuzzled my hand, making a small whining noise in his throat.

"There! See that?" Niles's voice held a note of triumph. "I told you people they'd remember." He saw both of us glance at the other dog. "Oh, shoot!" he said impatiently. "Soldier remembers, all right. You'd know it if he didn't. But he's been cocky all day, that one. Needs jackin' up, I can see that."

His voice sharpened. "Soldier, when I say

'friend,' you speak. Understand? She's a friend. Speak!"

The dog got to his feet and went through the required ritual. Then he sat back, great dark eyes alert as he looked at his master.

Praising them, Niles nodded to Peter and me, then disappeared into the shadows down the drive with both dogs at his heels.

For several moments, Peter stood leaning against one of the pillars by the front steps, looking off into the distance. Silence stretched between us, but I waited, knowing he would tell me in his own good time what he wanted me to know.

He said at last in a rigidly controlled voice, "Gretchen's fall was no accident, Alex."

I let out my breath in a soft sigh. "I suspected it wasn't."

"Someone stretched fishing line across the fourth step from the top of the stairs. So Gretchen fell. And she was hurt. But I can't help thinking it's possible — just barely — that someone tried to kill her."

My voice sounded hoarse. "But why? You're making a — an awfully serious accusation."

Peter shrugged. "It's an ugly thing to do, setting a trap like that. A fall down those stairs — well, you'd expect it to hurt someone badly, maybe — permanently."

"How did you know about the — the fishing line?"

"Found a piece of it caught in the carpeting.

And there are scratches in the varnish on the posts beneath the banister where it must have been tied. I'd swear that's how it was done."

"Doesn't Gretchen remember tripping over it?"

He shook his head. "She's drawn a complete blank. Doesn't recall falling or anything else until she came to with her head in Margaret's lap, Margaret's tears dripping down on her face. Maybe it's because she might have a slight concussion. So she doesn't remember what went before."

I thought for a moment. "You haven't told anybody but Hunter?"

"Haven't even told Gretchen. She'll undoubtedly figure it out when her head stops hurting." A pause. "How did you know I told Hunter?"

"Because something's bothering him a whole lot." I added crossly, "In his usual tactful way, he tried to get me to cancel out on the house party, or at least promise I'd leave once I'd talked to Gretchen. He said something's going on around here that he can't explain. Well, I knew that from the way Gretchen sounded on the phone."

"I'm on Hunt's side this time, Alex. Whatever the trouble is, it's serious. If he tried to keep you away, it's because somebody's already been hurt."

After furious thought, I asked him why he hadn't told the rest of the family that Gretchen's fall had been no accident. He was right, of course, when he said this thing was serious.

In the dim light, I couldn't read his expression. I could only see his sharp movement. "Hunt and I decided it might be better to keep quiet for a while, not scare off whoever's trying to — don't you see, Alex? If that person thinks we're writing it off as an accident, he'll try again. That may be our only hope of catching him. We're on guard now, watching everybody. That gives us an advantage."

It sounded reasonable. But as usual, I had to keep nibbling around the ragged edges. "Why did you tell me?"

He laughed, a short, brusque sound. "That's what Hunt's going to want to know," he said, his voice dry. "Partly because the most important thing is to keep anybody else from getting hurt. You're closer to Gretchen than — oh, Bonnie isn't apt to go poking around asking questions, trying to help. And Corey wouldn't pay attention if we warned him. He likes to play games. Guys like that — brains, but no *sense*. Listen, this situation could be dangerous. I mean that."

"Okay. You're right. So what else should I know?"

He sighed. "That's just it. We don't know an awful lot. Anybody could have tied that line across the stairs. Except for Dad and Grandpa. They were talking in Grandpa's room. I guess we can cross Alden and Margaret off the list, too, unless you're picky about husband-and-wife testimony. They say they were both in the kitchen getting lunch ready."

"So who does that leave?" I counted them off. "Niles and Kendall and Delphine and —"

"And Hunter," he said, his voice tired, "and me. And don't forget Bonnie and Corey if you want a complete list."

"Oh, it's impossible. I can't imagine anybody here doing such a thing." A small shiver traveled up my spine. "It just has to be somebody from outside."

"You know better than that. Niles keeps the gate locked, and the dogs are loose when he comes up to the house. No, Alex, it's one of us. It's somebody here at Meadowmount right now. Tonight."

I swallowed against a dry throat. Abruptly, something popped out of the confusion in my mind, a point not entirely clear. "Peter?" I turned the thought around and looked at it and said again, "Peter?"

"I haven't gone anywhere."

"Why are you so sure," I said slowly, "that this rotten little trap was set for Gretchen?"

"I like the way your mind works." But his voice sounded harsh. "A girl called this morning and asked for Gretchen. Margaret took the call in the downstairs hall, then went back to the kitchen to buzz Gretchen's room."

"But Gretchen came downstairs to answer?" I said, puzzled. "Oh. Sure. I can understand why she did that."

"You can?"

"Someone had been listening in on her calls. At least, they did the day she called me. I heard another phone hang up after she did."

"You sure?"

"Positive. So that might explain why she came downstairs. Right?"

A brief, humming silence. "No," Peter said. "Margaret wondered, too. Come to find out the phone in Gretchen's room is gone. It's on a jack, if you remember. So somebody was making sure she couldn't take the call up there."

"Who was calling?"

"Nobody knows. Margaret thinks it was a good ten minutes before she remembered she hadn't hung up the phone in the hall. She went to do it — and found Gretchen on the stairs."

I winced, picturing the scene all too clearly. Margaret, already under emotional strain, would have gone to pieces when she discovered Gretchen unconscious. No one would think about a phone off the hook for some time. Had that girl ever called back? Peter said no, not as far as he knew.

"It probably doesn't mean anything," I mused aloud.

Peter agreed. "Still, we've got a really muddled situation. Won't hurt to tie up all the loose ends we can. If I give you a list of Gretchen's friends, would you check to see if one of them called this morning?"

I groaned inwardly, thinking about the probable length of that list. But of course I agreed to help. "It's been quite a day," I said around a yawn. "I think I'll turn in. My brain's already punched the clock."

He laughed and leaned forward to touch my

shoulder. "Take care," he said, and his tone made it more than a meaningless comment.

I shivered as I went quickly across the entry hall and up the stairs, unable to keep from staring at the banister posts on either side of that fourth step from the top. Much as I loved Meadowmount, I couldn't help feeling an ominous change in the atmosphere.

For the first time beneath this roof, I was afraid.

4

A moment later in the upstairs hall, I passed
an open door and heard Grandpa Luther call
to me. I always thought of him by the name he
asked all the kids to use, protesting that Mr. von
Weber was entirely too formal.

He sat in his big leather chair by the window,
looking even smaller and more frail than I remembered. I'd never seen him wearing anything
but plain slacks and a long-sleeved plaid shirt,
switching from wool to cotton as his only conces-
sion to the season. One pocket bulged with pieces
of the hard peppermint candy he loved. Around
his neck was a worn bolo tie set with a silver
dollar.

"Here's my pretty Alex," he said with a chuckle.
Lamplight glinted from his glasses as he lifted his
cheek for me to kiss, reminding me of a child at

bedtime. The old, wrinkled cheek felt soft and cool. Thinning white hair hovered over his pink scalp, rather like the puff of a dandelion.

He gestured at the hearing aid in the bow of his glasses. "Good thing I hadn't gone off the air yet," he said. "I would have missed you."

"Grandpa Luther, it's great to see you again. You look just the same."

He nodded. "Been marking time for quite a spell," he said. "Figure I'm good for another six months, anyway. Now that I've seen men walking on the moon, I'd like to celebrate my hundredth birthday. And then — what's the expression you kids use?" He laughed. "Then I'll be ready to pack it in."

I grinned at him. "I never had any use for re-runs, either."

His faded blue eyes widened with delight, and he leaned forward to put a hand on my arm. "Do you know, you're the first person with sense enough to see that? Alex, I hope you'll stay awhile." He seemed to droop in the echo of the words. The light went out of his face, and his mouth trembled.

"What is it?" I asked, alarmed.

His hand patted mine. "Nothing, child. It's just that things aren't the same these days. Meadowmount used to be a happy place." His head moved slowly, painfully. Then he sat for several seconds, motionless, staring at the opposite wall.

I resisted the impulse to turn and look myself. Urgently, I searched for something to say that might pull him back to his former cheerful mood. "It was wonderful to see Peter Braun again. He says his father's here, too. Did he bring you news from your old partner?" The moment the words were out of my mouth, I wished I could recall them. I remembered then that Herman Braun had died before I met the von Webers. He, too, had lived to his mid-nineties.

Grandpa saw my expression and dismissed my embarrassment with a slight gesture. "I'll be bringing *him* the news one of these days, I expect. Oh, we both had a run for our money, that's for sure. Death isn't any tragedy at my age, sweetheart. Once I get things straightened out around here" — he hesitated, then smiled up at me once more — "I'll go on to new adventures without any regrets."

I bent down to kiss him again. I had always loved this old man, pleased and astonished at how easily we'd been able to span the years between us to find common ground. Grandpa read a great deal, and he'd retained his interest in people, observing both good and bad traits in those around him with amused tolerance.

He said now in a half-whisper, "Why don't you peek in on Gretchen? I've got a hunch she's not going to get more than a few catnaps tonight. Couldn't give her anything to help her sleep, not with a head injury."

I looked at him, startled. How had he found out about Gretchen's fall? Then I remembered he always had seemed to know what went on at

Meadowmount, though nobody ever admitted telling him of unpleasant incidents.

He caught my look. "Pshaw!" he said. "Of course I know what happened. Poor little girl." He shook his head, looking both sad and irritated. "Not that anyone ever wants to tell me anything. Trying to spare me, that's what they think they're doing. Know what that means? Isolation. And who wants to end up in a cocoon? Listen, child, life begins in the womb with isolation. Nobody in his right mind wants to go back to that."

His eyes gleamed with humor. "The good Lord's seen fit to spare my senses so far. Must be some reason for that."

I felt inordinately pleased to be able to leave him smiling. In my room, I found all the lamps burning. Seconds after I closed the door, I heard Gretchen call to me.

A dim nightlight by her bed gave off a rosy radiance. When I tiptoed in, she touched the switch, then squinted in the sudden glare. She lay flat on her back without a pillow under her head. Only her eyes moved for a moment. Then she smiled.

"Hi," she said in a small voice. "You're even prettier than you used to be. How do you do it? Oh, Alex, I'm so glad to see you."

She looked exactly the same except that her round face was flushed, her short, shaggy hair a bit tousled. In rumpled pink pajamas, she looked like a sleepy little kid.

I told her so, gave her a cautious kiss on the

cheek, and sat down on the chair beside her bed. "I was hoping you could sleep. How's your head?"

She made a face. "It may roll off any minute, and good riddance. Oh, I don't think it's too serious. I'm just not going to have much fun for a couple of days. I slept a little, but now I think I'll try to stay awake for a while. Maybe I can get through the night better."

"Are you sure? We can talk in the morning."

"I'm okay if I don't move. Just sort of woolly-headed." She gave me a crooked smile. "Peter's going to have a great time telling me all the nutty things I said and did. Already I remember babbling in his ear when he carried me upstairs. Something about somebody trying to kill me. Did you ever hear anything so — ?" She stopped, closed her eyes, and took a quick breath, almost a gasp.

"Well, what do you know?" The words were light, but her tone was not. She opened her eyes. "Peter said it might come back like that, all of a sudden." Her hand groped for mine and clutched it. It was as if she needed something solid to hang onto.

"There was — I *didn't* trip. And I didn't get dizzy and black out. Alex, I fell over something." She let go of my hand to point at her feet. "Pull down the sheet and look at my leg. Not the one with the ace bandage. Guess I sprained that ankle. It's the other leg. See what I mean?"

I did. There was a red line across her shin, the skin actually broken at the point where the bone was closest to the surface.

Wide brown eyes searched my face. "What was it?" she asked.

I hesitated for only a second. "Fishing line. Peter found a scrap of it caught in the carpeting."

Her face contorted in the fierce grimace that meant she was thinking hard. When she spoke, it sounded as if she were talking to herself. "It's — in the air around here. Everybody's acting so weird. And Grandpa's been in a real flap. That scared me more than anything, you know? I didn't think anybody on the planet could rattle Grandpa. And mysterious phone calls. Long distance, any hour of the night. Even a letter, special delivery. That's a laugh, up here in God's backyard, right?"

Peter had been sure she would put it all together once her head felt better. I watched and listened as she did just that.

She addressed the ceiling in slow, halting phrases. "I put in a call, myself. To Peter. My rock, the source of all wisdom." An exasperated sound. "I'm sure he knows something about — whatever it is that's going on. But he won't talk. If I weren't so crazy about him, I'd — I'd wring his scrawny neck."

I smiled. "His neck's as gorgeous as the rest of him. And he's just as crazy about you. But I know what you mean. When he filled me in, I figured he knew more than he wanted to say right then. That's the way Peter is, Gretchen. You know him better than anybody. If he's not sure about something, he clams up."

"*Tell* me about it," she said, resigned. "His father coming with him — that was odd, too. Peter admits that much, that he doesn't know of any particular reason, I mean. And Grandpa Luther — Alex, you know I'm closer to him than I am to my father, or ever was to my grandparents. Just as close as I am to Hunt, though in a different way. What I'm trying to say is — I can tell when something shakes him up pretty good. And that's the way he's acting now. But he's not issuing orders — *wham! bang! zappo!* — like a five-star general, shaping everybody up like he always did before when a crisis came along. That's what — that's what scares me."

I nodded. During our brief conversation, Grandpa certainly had acted strangely. It bothered me, too.

Gretchen flung out her hands, then winced at the sudden movement. "But why all the mystery? If it's something about the Sunrise, doesn't that concern the whole family? Besides, you'd think by now everybody'd said all they had to say about our sacred Sunrise."

I must have looked confused. Gretchen made a more cautious gesture toward her grandfather's room and explained, "The insurance companies have a fit every so often because Grandpa insists on keeping the Sunrise here. I told you about that once, how he had the walls built and got the dogs, all the security nonsense. None of it changed their attitude one bit. They keep raising the policy rates. About two months ago, Grandpa pitched a curve of his own and canceled everything."

She gave me her impish grin. "Corey's father has an insurance agency, you know. So Corey's been camping on our doorstep lately, buddying up to Grandpa. I suppose he's trying to talk Grandpa into signing another policy with his dad. People around here know it would be next to impossible to break into this place. So — more power to him."

"Mmmm," I said and studied her. She looked tired, eyes glazed with pain. "Gretchen, let's save the rest until tomorrow. I think you should try to sleep. I've had a pretty full day, too."

"Okay." She didn't try to argue. "I just wanted you to know that — I'm really frightened now. I could have broken my neck falling down those stairs. Maybe somebody planned it that way. And the other stuff — I can't seem to get through to Peter or Hunt that it's *serious*. At least they won't talk to me. And Grandpa's already got something on his mind —"

"How about your father?"

She made a face. "Dad lives in another world, always has. I discovered early — I was four, I think — that fathers are not for helping. Or for solving problems. Not this one, anyway. And Delphine's never been a big favorite of mine, either. I went round and round till I thought about you. How I could always trust you with a secret and — Alex, I knew you'd come if I said I needed you. I wasn't kidding. You can see that now. So you'll stay and help, won't you?"

She knew me well enough to know I'd find it impossible to refuse. I wondered even then, though, whether the ugly situation, still a mystery to both of us, had already gone past the point where anybody could control it.

I was so tired, the questions in my mind didn't keep me awake for long after my head hit the pillow. I woke only once, probably several hours later, to hear a phone ringing shrilly through the silent house.

Must be in the room below me, I thought drowsily, or down the long corridor in the other wing. Not in Gretchen's room. Someone had taken her phone. . . .

5

The next morning brought brilliant sunshine and a feeling of foreboding like the heaviness preceding a headache. I lay for several minutes wondering if it had been a mistake to come again to Meadowmount. Then, remembering Gretchen's small face, the note of fear in her voice, and the pain she was suffering so stoically, I felt ashamed of myself.

When I cautiously opened the door off our connecting bath, I found her waiting for me. This time, she sat propped against her pillows.

"I thought you'd never wake up," she said impatiently. "Breakfast's coming on trays for both of us. Now sit down and let me test your powers of observation. What's different about this room from the way it was last night?"

"You're sitting up. Is your head better? Did you sleep?"

"Yes to everything, thanks." She pointed to the chair beside her, still with the air of suppressed excitement. "But I'm not talking about something different about me."

Obediently, I sat and studied the room, taking my time about it. Gretchen had done her bedroom in pale green and yellow. The bed, dresser, and desk were of maple, matching a small rocker, a desk chair, and the chair I sat in. There were two bedside tables, lamps with yellow bases, a reading lamp on her desk and . . .

"Your phone's back!" I exclaimed. "It wasn't there last night. Peter said somebody took it. . . ."

"You're sharp, all right." Gretchen smiled at me, then sobered abruptly. "I've been sitting here putting more pieces together. Somebody swiped my phone, so when that call came and Margaret buzzed, I had to go downstairs to answer.

"Delphine's been locking her sitting-room door lately. Paranoid, as usual. She thinks the cleaning woman's been helping herself to a few things in there. And Grandpa was busy with Mr. Braun. So neither of those phones were available." She raised her eyebrows. "Incidentally, did anybody ever find out who called me?"

I told her Peter had asked me to check it out.

She made a vague gesture. "Bonnie can help. The girl's a bloodhound. Besides, she's after Hunter." She added, her voice casual, "Is that all right with you?"

I met her gaze, hoping nothing on my face revealed my reaction to her question. Naturally,

Gretchen had been aware that I was wild about her brother years before. I swore her to secrecy at the time, so I was positive she hadn't let Hunter know how I felt. "Sure, that's okay," I said. "Why not?"

Gretchen sighed. "I was afraid you'd say that."

A tap on the door signaled Margaret's arrival with our breakfast trays. She arranged mine in front of me and put Gretchen's on one of those sickbed contraptions with two short legs to keep it level.

Then, hands on her hips, the housekeeper looked at us. She wore her wavy gray hair short and parted on the side, clipped with a mother-of-pearl barrette. Gretchen told me once that Margaret had worn her hair the same way as long as anyone could remember. Yesterday and today, I noticed she wore dark pantsuits instead of the severe, unadorned dresses of years ago, possibly because they looked like uniforms.

"You've always been such a healthy child," she said to Gretchen. "I don't believe anyone has used this bed tray since your mother died. But are you sure you should be sitting up?"

"My head's okay except for a kind of dull feeling," Gretchen assured her. "It's sore, but the ice took down a lot of the swelling. You're a great nurse, Margaret."

The housekeeper looked pleased. She fussed with the bedding for a moment. "Would your ankle feel better if you had it on a pillow?"

"No, it'll be fine if I don't move around too much."

Margaret's mouth firmed. "Then you stay in bed today. Promise me."

"Nope, I can't promise anything. If the house catches on fire, I don't want to feel honor bound to fry, ankle and all. . . ."

"Don't say such things! Don't even think such things!" Margaret departed, still sputtering.

For me, the flurry of activity had been a welcome interruption. I didn't want to talk about Hunter or my dismay to find that nothing had changed in two years. I still went rubber-kneed and hollow inside when he was around, and he still acted as if I were thirteen with bangs and braids and braces on my teeth.

As we ate, I deliberately changed the subject, telling Gretchen about the anonymous letters Bonnie and I had received. I told her, too, that someone had listened in on our conversation the day she called.

Gretchen nodded. "Doesn't surprise me. It's been going on for weeks." She scowled. "It's a dirty, sneaky business, for sure. Somebody in my own home, someone here at Meadowmount, maybe one of the family — it makes me sick, Alex." She said after a moment. "I'd like to see that letter. Did you bring it with you?"

"Yes, I thought you'd want to see it." I saw her expression. "Don't worry, it's safe. I locked it in my vanity case." I went to get the small square case from the closet shelf and fished the key out of my bag before I went back to Gretchen's room. I didn't notice the scratch marks around the lock until I realized the key wouldn't turn.

Someone had pried the case open. The letter was gone.

Gretchen took one look at my face and shook her head. "Figures," she said, her voice grim. "Now it's only your word for it — unless Bonnie brought her letter, too, and found a better hiding place. Did they ruin the lock, forcing it open?"

"Oh, it doesn't matter," I lied. "It's an old thing, anyway." But I sure wouldn't be able to repair or replace it in a hurry, I thought sadly. And remembered how thrilled I'd been when my parents gave it to me for my twelfth birthday. I didn't tell Gretchen that. She'd feel even worse than I did.

"Gretchen, we'll find out what's going on, somehow. Peter says to be careful, but — once we know why these things are happening, maybe we can figure out who's doing them."

I didn't add that I had an uncomfortable feeling of urgency. What if Gretchen were in even greater danger now? Was time a factor? The person who set that trap for her might already realize that we knew about the fishline strung across the stairs. They'd know we'd be suspicious, on guard the moment we discovered the latest incident, the theft of the letter from my vanity case.

"The Braun family's involved somehow," Gretchen said, looking thoughtful, "or why would Peter's father be here? Will you try to pump Grandpa today, Alex? He's always liked you. Get him talking about the good old days with Herman Braun. Maybe he'll let something slip."

"I'll try."

"And I bet it's got something to do with the Sunrise, too. Can't prove it, but — every time there's any trouble around here that blasted necklace is at the bottom of it. Isn't it sad when something that beautiful makes so much trouble in a family?"

I moved the breakfast trays to her desk, then perched on one corner and stared at her. "You mean you think someone wants to *steal* it?"

Gretchen leaned back against her pillows. "I'll put it this way. Everybody in this house wants something really bad. And maybe they could get that something, whatever it is that's so important to them, if they had the Sunrise. To sell or use, whatever. . . ."

She tapped one index finger against the other, ticking off members of the household. "If I start with the least likely people — well, Niles Benson wants a spread of his own, somewhere away from everyone, naturally, and before he's too old to enjoy it. Alden and Margaret? Well, there's the thing with the twin sister, paying off the smuggler — did Hunter tell you about that?"

"No, but Peter did."

"Mmm. Are you aware that Peter resents the Sunrise? Oh, bitterly! In fact, it affects the way he feels about my whole clan. The fact that Grandpa owns that necklace, well, it helps obscure the fact that Peter's great-grandfather was at least as remarkable as Luther von Weber. Whenever Grandpa talks about their adventures in

Alaska, you'll notice he always says, 'It took two of us.' "

She leaned forward. "It's the mystique business that turns me off. Hunter, too. The Sunrise is famous all over the world, but almost nobody knows about the wonderful feeling between those two men. There wouldn't have been any magnificent art treasure if it hadn't been for Herman Braun making a special trip to China and finding the incredible family that made the Sunrise. For that matter, if it hadn't been for him, there wouldn't be any Luther von Weber. Herman saved his life once, you know. Later, Grandpa returned the favor twice over. So it did take two of them, all right."

She gave a short laugh. "Anyway. Dad's furious with Grandpa for even hinting he might give the Sunrise to a museum. Dad doesn't care about its value in dollars and cents. With him, it *is* the whole silly thing that's built up around a necklace that's one of a kind, priceless in every sense." She rolled her eyes. "Delphine feels the same way, only more so. With her, money always matters."

She went on after a moment. "Now that I'm not a little kid anymore, Grandpa talks to me a lot about the family. He opens up more, especially about mistakes he thinks he made. He and Grandma Caroline were so wrapped up with each other, they never became very close to their son. That's my Grandpa Joe — you've never met him.

He and Grandma Sue live up north in one of those retirement places.

"Well, Dad's exactly like his father — everybody says so. And you know Dad isn't a warm person, never has been. But I always tell Grandpa, maybe it worked out okay. Dad and Delphine seem happy enough. Neither of them are loving people. But my mother was. So Hunter and I had one parent to pattern ourselves after — and Grandpa, of course."

She added softly, "If you have somebody, just one person who cares about you and knows you and takes you the way you really are, that's enough, I think. If you have more than one person like that, it's just fabulous luck. I had Mom and Grandpa and Hunt — and terrific friends like you — and now there's Peter, too."

I smiled at her, realizing once more how lucky I'd been to have marvelous parents. Long ago, I learned that the von Weber children's view of their father and stepmother was surprisingly objective. Gretchen's mother had died seven years ago. When Kendall married Delphine two years later, Gretchen admitted candidly, she and Hunter loathed their stepmother on sight. She added, a gleam in her brown eyes, that the feeling had been mutual.

As time went on, they kept out of each other's way, not a difficult thing to do in this vast house. Margaret ran the household for the most part. She adored Gretchen, and I suspected that eased the problem. I doubted that anything could ruffle

Delphine, certainly nothing as minor as a couple of stepchildren who detested her.

A rap at the door interrupted my thoughts. I opened it to find Hunter and Peter in the hall. Their cheerful greetings sounded a little strained. Neither of them looked as if they'd slept well.

Peter went immediately to kiss Gretchen. Holding her hand, he stared down at her for several moments. "How do you feel today?"

"Much better." Gretchen widened her eyes at him. "But you look awful. Didn't you sleep at all?"

Peter shrugged and turned to sprawl in the chair beside her bed, legs stretched out in front of him. "I spent the night in the hall outside your door. No, don't say it. I got more sleep that way than if I'd been in bed on the other side of the house, worrying."

So it hadn't been my hyper imagination, I thought. Peter seemed to feel the same apprehension about the possibility of lingering danger to Gretchen.

Hunter watched me, his eyes moody. "How much has she figured out?" he asked quietly.

But Gretchen heard him. "Everything," she said, "except why anybody'd want to do something so rotten — and who it was — and why they picked on adorable me." Despite the light words, her voice wavered a little. "Alex and I were talking about that phone call yesterday and — hey, you guys, somebody brought my phone back last night." She paused, staring at Peter.

"But I thought you said you slept outside my door —"

"I didn't come on duty till eleven. You were probably asleep by then. But the phone doesn't matter that much. It would have turned up sooner or later, hidden away somewhere. And how could we prove anything with it?"

Gretchen sighed. "Whoever's doing this seems to stay — invisible. Tell them about the anonymous letter, Alex."

Conscious of Hunter's gaze, I looked at Peter as I explained.

He made a harsh sound. "Can't blame you for thinking it was safe. Hunt and I both assumed we could wait for a few hours last night before we set up surveillance on this end of the house. Figured it might be wise to keep an eye on the first floor, too. We were wrong on both counts." He got up and walked to the window to stand for a moment looking down into the rose garden, fists jammed into his pockets.

Hunter said, his voice tight, "As it turns out, we were mistaken about something else. Maybe we guarded the wrong people."

Gretchen and I glanced at each other, then at him.

"Peter's father," Hunter said. "He's gone, along with his luggage. Car's gone, too. He knew Peter was staying on, but — he didn't even leave a note to explain why he split in the middle of the night. And nobody saw him leave. Nobody heard a thing."

"Oh, Peter!" Gretchen stretched out her hand to him. "Peter, you don't think — that something's *happened* to him?"

He turned, his face a mask except for his dark, burning eyes. "Yes," he said, "that's exactly what I think."

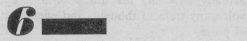

6

Gretchen and Peter talked for several moments, heads close, their voices low and tense. As I watched, I decided it might be a good time to talk to Grandpa. He'd undoubtedly been up for hours, an early riser since the days when Meadowmount was a working ranch.

I hesitated, however, trying to think of some way to get him talking about the old days in Alaska. Then I remembered he'd once promised to let me tape some of his stories. I'd wanted them at the time just because they were so interesting. Now I realized I could use them for school, too. The English and journalism teachers at Bonita Vista High liked material based on the memories and experiences of early settlers in San Diego County.

"Hunter, do you have a tape recorder I can borrow?"

He looked at me blankly. "Sure. But Gretch has one in her desk." He opened a drawer and took it out along with a new cassette. "This okay?"

I nodded. "Thanks." If he hadn't been studying me, curious, I might have explained why I wanted it. But on the rare occasions when he actually gave me his full attention, I lost my voice, my train of thought, and every last vestige of poise.

No, I'm not usually that unsophisticated. And Hunter isn't the only guy around, either, merely the only one I care about. I thought crossly, *It would have been better for me if I'd never laid eyes on him.* For four years, I'd compared every boy I met with Hunter von Weber, and they all failed to measure up.

When I opened the door to the corridor, I heard men's voices, the sound of hammering, then the high whine of a drill. The men must have arrived to install the chair elevator, I thought. The von Weber name had certainly produced fast service.

In the doorway to Grandpa's room, I stopped, alarmed to see the old man in his chair, head back, his eyes closed, and the slight figure so still that my heart froze within me.

"Grandpa Luther!" My voice emerged in a hoarse croak. "Grandpa, are you all right?"

There was no response. But when I hurried to him and touched his hand, he stirred, blinking up at me. Then he smiled and touched the bow of his glasses. "Sorry, dear, didn't hear you. With all that racket out there, I went off the air. Must have dozed for a minute."

Before I could hide them, he saw the tears in my eyes. "Sweet Alex, would you cry for me?"

In his wispy voice, it sounded like the words to an old song, the kind Hunter would call "a moldy oldie." *Stop thinking about Hunter*, I told myself sternly.

I bent to kiss Grandpa's cheek. "I'll cry, all right," I said with a shaky laugh, "but it won't be for you. It'll be for the rest of us. We'll sure miss you."

He said with a trace of his impish humor, "Glad to hear that. You're better than a tonic, child. You and Gretchen —" He squeezed my hand. "Maybe we can straighten things out yet, make it like it used to be here at Meadowmount."

I heard the plea in his voice, saw it in the eyes that had watched history in the making. It broke my heart to think of anything troubling him so deeply in the last chapter of his life. It made me furious, too, reinforcing my resolve to help him as well as Gretchen in any way I could.

"We'll try. We'll sure try." I wondered again how much Grandpa knew about Gretchen's fall and the other ugly incidents.

"A person should try everything," he said softly. "When things go wrong, as they are in this house right this minute, why, you have to do all you can. Isn't that so?"

I had to lean close to hear the words. It was

as if he were talking to himself in the way some elderly people had. But never this one. A moment later, he peered at me, waiting for my reply.

"Yes," I said, "a person should do everything possible to make things right." A solemn pledge, absurd and emotional, but the moment called for it and so did he. And I loved this old man.

He sighed and patted my hand. Then he noticed the tape recorder I'd put on the round table beside his chair. He chuckled. "Last time you came to visit, you wanted to get me on tape. Imagine you remembering that after two whole years."

I felt my face flush, hating the necessity to be devious about my request.

Grandpa happily suggested that I shut the door and set up the recorder. Once I had it going, I handed him the small microphone and asked, "Could we begin with the way you met your partner on the boat? On the *City of Seattle*, going up to Alaska?"

Surprisingly, he shook his head. "No," he said, his voice firm. "This isn't a good day for remembering our gold mine — and all the luck that came of it. Bad as well as good." He looked out the window for a moment, as if he were gazing into the past. "Let me tell you how I crossed the country, about the wagon I built."

It held all the worldly goods of a boy who had been a little younger than I, a boy determined to seek his fortune on the country's west frontier. He packed that wagon with a few clothes, a bed, a stove, and the plow his brother-in-law had given him in lieu of wages for working in his store.

"I had a team of horses," he said, "and harness that was almost new. Couple of mares, Nellie and Maud. They were all that was left when my father's affairs were settled.

"By rights, my sister was entitled to half the estate, but she was married by then to the town druggist. Miserly sort, he was. Didn't have need of another horse, but he figured on selling it. Sister said, no such thing, she wanted to give that horse to me. Nearly broke her heart that she couldn't do more."

He sat for a moment, plainly recalling that painful scene, as the recorder hummed in the silence.

When he glanced at me again, I tried to nudge him forward in his narrative. "Had your partner, Herman Braun, come over from Germany at this point? Was he already out on the West Coast?"

It didn't work. He waved the questions away. "That came later," he said. "I used to tell this story to Gretchen and Hunter when they were little. None of you will ever see your country as I saw it on that trip. Flat prairie, never touched by a plow, as far as the eye could see, day after day. It was like crossing an ocean of grass. I might have been the first white man to come that way.

"Out there in the middle of nothing, I came across a little settlement, just a stable and a boarding house and a country store. People were raising wheat thereabouts, and I thought about my plow and debated if I should stay."

He shook his head. "But when I had supper with those folks, I could tell there was something wrong, tension in the air. Couldn't understand it. I knew they had room, but they told me I couldn't sleep in the house. Said if I wanted to stay, I'd have to bed down in the stable. They'd give me clean straw, they said. So that's what I elected to do."

He touched his cheek with fingers that shook slightly. "In the middle of the night, I heard a commotion outside and got up to look out the door. You know what I saw, Alex? Vigilantes. Every man jack of them with a six-shooter in his belt. And there was a dead man in the wagon, the rope still around his neck."

I held my breath, picturing that horrid scene. "What did you do?" I asked in a near whisper.

He chuckled. "Same question all my kids used to ask," he said. "I'll tell you what I told them. I did what any sensible man would do in such a situation. I went back to my straw bed and back to sleep."

Again, his faded eyes looked into the distant past. "I ask myself now," he said slowly, "was that the right thing I did? I was a boy then, alone and more scared than I wanted to admit. But, Alex, I still wonder. Is it wise to mix in somebody else's affairs? There's a part in every man that likes to play God, I guess. Even when we call it by every other name under the sun, that's what it boils down to."

Was he speaking of the present as well as the past? The silence stretched. At last I risked another question. "What did you do the next morning? The morning after you saw the vigilantes?"

With an obvious effort, he shook off his heavy thoughts and gave me a pale smile. "I was mighty relieved to see things had cooled down," he said. "No sign of the night visitors. I tell you, it didn't take me long to change my mind about staying around those parts. I hightailed it out of there without even waiting long enough for breakfast."

"And then you headed for Alaska?"

The old man laughed aloud. "You're just like Gretchen and Hunter. When they were little, they'd sit at my feet, eyes as big as silver dollars. And they'd say, 'Hurry up, Gramp, get to the Alaska part!' "

His eyes twinkled with the mischief I had found irresistible from the first day I met him. "All in good time," he said. "Don't you want to hear about the crop of wheat I planted to earn my passage on the *City of Seattle*?"

At that point, he knew very well I was anxious for him to get to the Alaskan part of his tale. But I sensed more than mischief in the way he put me off. For some reason, Grandpa Luther seemed reluctant to discuss that particular adventure. I supposed it was due in part to Mr. Braun's abrupt departure last night under curious circumstances. Grandpa must be worrying about that, of course.

Someone rapped on the door. As I switched off the recorder, Hunter came in with Niles Benson.

The caretaker's nondescript face showed no emotion. But when he spoke, he didn't try to conceal the irritation in his voice. "Mr. von Weber, I really can't tell you anything about Mr. Braun leaving last night. You know this kind of thing has happened before. And it will again unless I'm told specifically to watch that gate every minute after sundown. Someone can slip by quite easily if they're familiar with the mechanism. And if the dogs know them."

"Calm down, Niles," the old man said, his voice quiet. "Nobody's blaming you for anything. We aren't sure yet just what happened except that Mr. Braun must have gone through that gate when he left."

I started to get up, thinking they might want to discuss the matter in private. But Grandpa touched my arm and shook his head, so I leaned back in my chair again.

Hunter walked to the window, then turned, hands in the back pockets of his Levis, dark eyes thoughtful. "Why don't you tell him the way you piece it together, Niles?"

Niles sighed. "Well, just after I got out of the shower — about eleven o'clock that was — I thought I heard a car. Went to look a few minutes later, but I didn't see anything out of the way. Gate was closed, but you house people would do that, going out. At that hour, it's only locked from the outside. Any of you coming back would have your key. Or you'd honk to be let in if you'd forgot it. In any case, I went to bed and thought no more about it."

Grandpa nodded, a shadow on his face. When he made a vague gesture, Niles must have taken it for dismissal. The old man watched him leave, his eyes unhappy. He had not been entirely distracted by our talk about the past, I thought. But then, neither had I.

After several moments, Hunter came to put a hand on his grandfather's shoulder. "What do you think, Grandpa? Is that what happened? Did Peter's father have a reason for leaving like that, without saying a word to anyone? Was he ticked off about something?"

Silence. At length, a long sigh. "Yes," Grandpa said. "He was — upset, all right. So was I. But, Hunter, you must see the puzzling part of this. Walter Braun would not leave this house like a thief in the night, without a word. He's a proper sort, Walter is. Raised that way, almost stuffy about good manners, that kind of thing. Same as your father, boy."

He muttered almost under his breath, "Must skip a generation, now and again." Then, firmly, "Why, Walter Braun could no more pack his bags and leave in the middle of the night than — than I'd visit the governor in my nightshirt. No!"

His voice, belligerent in denial, echoed through the room.

"No?" Hunter repeated. "What do you mean, no?"

His grandfather glared at him. "I mean, *no, that's not what happened!*" There was surprising strength in his voice, a hint of the powerful man he had once been.

"But you just said — you told Niles that Mr. Braun went through the front gate when he left."

"Yes, I think he did. His car's gone, isn't it? But I don't think he was alone, and I don't think he wanted to leave. Dammit, boy, I can't say it much plainer than that. It's there for anyone to see if they look hard enough. Somebody took Walter away last night. And if we haven't heard anything from him by this time — and we haven't — what other answer is there? Something's happened to him."

As we stared at him, he turned to look out the window. His mouth trembled for a moment, but his voice was low and steady. "I think somebody wanted Walter out of the way. I think he may be dead."

Clearly, he'd forgotten I was there, listening to words that made my blood run cold. I couldn't bear to look at him, my throat aching with a reflection of the pain in his voice. I found myself staring at a painting on the wall above his head. Grandpa's beloved Caroline smiled back at me, serene and lovely in a white dress, her dark hair piled high on her small head.

There, against the flawless, rose-tinted skin, low on her slender neck, was the Alaskan Sunrise, a glowing pectoral. Dozens of carved, linked animals hung from four strands of woven gold rope. The artist had captured the intricate pattern of each golden figure, highlighting the jeweled eyes and delicate insets of jade.

Again, I heard the echo of Gretchen's wistful voice. *"Isn't it sad when something that beautiful makes so much trouble in a family?"*

7

Hunter's face tightened. Squatting down beside his grandfather's chair, he looked directly into the old man's face.

"What do you mean, he may be dead? You've got to tell me, Gramp. What happened between the two of you? What's going on? Look, you must have some idea who took Mr. Braun out of here."

Grandpa Luther did not respond, except for a glance at me and a faint sigh. It said clearly that I'd been right. For a minute or two, all during the tense discussion about Peter's father, Grandpa had forgotten that I was there.

Hunter said urgently, "Don't you realize, if you're right about Mr. Braun, *you* could be in danger, too? Listen, I'm not being melodramatic about all this. Someone else has already been hurt."

"My little Gretchen. I know."

His grandson looked startled. He stood up then and flung out his hands in a gesture of total frustration. "Well, then?"

I interrupted, cutting across the sharp question, noting the weariness on Grandpa's face. "Not now, Hunter. He's had about all he can take."

Dark eyes glared at me. "He's insisting that somebody took Peter's father out of here — against his will. Not only that. He says he thinks Mr. Braun may be dead. He can't drop a bomb like that and —"

Grandpa Luther lifted one hand in an imperious gesture that stopped Hunter in mid-sentence. "Yes, I can," he said, but his voice was mild. "At the moment, there's nothing we can do about Walter — or anything else. We can't report Walter missing for at least twenty-four hours. All we can do is wait. There isn't any sense running around in circles, getting all riled up about it. I said what I did with good reason, Hunter, to put you on guard. Now that I've done that, I don't aim to say another word."

He flicked the tiny switch on his hearing aid and leaned back, eyes closed, hands folded across his thin chest. They were beautiful old hands, blue veins prominent, a simple gold wedding band riding almost to the knuckle in a groove worn by the years.

Studying those hands and the deliberate repose of the thin, ascetic face about them, I felt again a mixture of strong emotions. Affection for this old man mingled with outrage that his life and his household should be disturbed by something so destructive.

I stopped to examine the word. Yes, someone at Meadowmount was destroying the happiness and serenity of Grandpa's last days. I couldn't even think about that without feeling the heat of anger. If we could restore those things to him — but the only way to do that was to find out who was responsible for Gretchen's fall and Mr. Braun's disappearance.

Hunter followed me out of the room, then put one hand on my shoulder, turning me to face him. "Do you see now why I asked you to cancel out on this visit? I don't want you mixed up in whatever it is that's going on around here. Can't you understand that?"

I stared at him, aware of his touch, almost holding my breath. For a moment, I thought he might really care about me.

Then, as I watched, his face went through the quicksilver change unique to him when he's under stress. It's like a shrug, a split second of animation with a subtle difference in expression once his face is still again. This time, it meant that the look of concern disappeared, replaced by an easy and totally phony smile.

"Hey," he said softly, "be reasonable. Pete and I can take care of Gretchen. Sooner or later, we're going to find out who's behind this crazy business."

I thought crossly, they hadn't done such a great job last night, either in taking care of people or unraveling the mystery. No, it hadn't been their fault. They simply couldn't be everywhere in this vast house at the same time.

That was enough reason for me to resist the logic in what Hunter said, as well as his implied request. Obviously, he thought I'd be doing everybody a great big favor if I went home. The super-capable guys on the premises could then proceed with the investigation, unhampered by this particular silly, stubborn female. A kid, at that.

Hunter must have read most of what I was thinking on my face. If he'd picked up only a tenth of my reaction, I suspect it would have been sufficient.

"Okay, I tried," he said in a resigned tone. "Will you stay close to Gretchen, then? It'll make it easier, and it may be safer for both of you."

"All right," I said and watched him stride down the hall. When I glanced again through the open bedroom door, I had to laugh.

Grandpa Luther sat looking at me, a beatific smile on his face. Then he nodded, looking pleased, and leaned back once more.

No wonder he knew about everything that went on in this house, I thought, amused. I went down the hall, but paused in front of Gretchen's room when I heard Bonnie Layton's voice within. At the moment, I desperately needed to sort out my thoughts. And as long as Gretchen wasn't alone. . . . Maybe some fresh air would help clear the muddle in my head.

Picking my way past the men working on the chair elevator, I reflected wryly that Delphine would be pleased with their work. There was not a mark on the beautiful old banisters that Margaret kept polished to a high gloss.

I headed outdoors and around the house to the rose garden. In the center was a small tiled patio, a fishpond, chairs, and a chaise lounge.

Too late, I saw Corey's blond head. He turned as he heard me approach, gray eyes alight with a smile that said I was precisely the person he wanted to see.

Then he said it aloud, sounding pleased. "I've been waiting for you. Knew you'd have to get out of the house after a while, with all the weird things that have been happening. Figured you might come out here."

I smiled at him. "Good figuring." Then his words registered. "You've heard about Mr. Braun?"

"Yes." He got to his feet, motioned me to take the lounge, then dragged up a chair beside me. "Delphine just gave me coffee and doughnuts along with her version of what actually took place."

"And that was — ?"

He shook his head, thick blond hair glinting in the bright sunlight. "She thinks somebody's making a 'mountain out of a mouse hole.'" He quoted her with obvious relish.

"How does she explain the way Mr. Braun took off without saying a word, not even leaving a note to say why? Grandpa Luther says it isn't a bit like him. He'd know more about that than Delphine, wouldn't he?"

Corey looked thoughtful as he massaged the ankle of the foot propped across his knee. "That's just it," he said. "Delphine claims Mr. Braun told her when he got here that he might have to leave suddenly. She said he apologized in advance in case it happened that way. Ergo, no Mount Everest, only a mouse hole."

I winced. "No, it merely brings it down to a question of — whom you believe. Sorry, I'd rather take Peter's word that it isn't that simple. And Grandpa's. For one thing, they know Mr. Braun better than Delphine does. And for another —" I stopped short of saying that they both knew something else, the true reason Mr. Braun had come down to see Grandpa.

But Corey echoed the words stuck on the tip of my tongue. "And for another, both Peter and Mr. von Weber know the reason why Mr. Braun made this sudden mysterious visit to Meadowmount. Isn't that right?"

I stared at him.

"Oh, it isn't any secret that it's a mystery," he said. "He hasn't been down here in ten years, Delphine says. She's really upset about the whole thing. Goes back a few months, you know. That's when Mr. von Weber began making noises about giving the Alaskan Sunrise to a museum. She blames the Braun family. Don't ask me why."

Abruptly, something surfaced that had puzzled me last night, though I hadn't really paused to think about it. "Is it my imagination, or are Kendall and Delphine acting a little cool toward Peter?"

Corey grinned. "Cold would be a better word for it. It's only lately that it stopped being cool, however. He and Gretchen were never as close as they are now. I guess you don't realize there's never been much love lost between the two families, not since the original partners." He shrugged. "Jealousy, probably. Luther von Weber has the Sunrise, and all the fame and honor and glory came to him. Does anybody ever hear anything about Herman Braun? Or whoever his son was? Or Walter, either, for that matter?"

I sighed. "Everything that happens — it comes right back to the Sunrise."

"For sure," Corey said softly. "Everybody's interested in that little trinket, for one reason or another."

I glanced at him. "Probably we're the only people around here who don't have any — ah — personal interest in it." I remembered then what Gretchen had told me, that recently Corey seemed very interested, indeed, on behalf of his father's insurance agency.

The gray eyes flickered with amusement, as if he had read my mind. "Thanks for the vote of confidence. I'll have to confess that my father would like the insurance package. He'd like that a lot."

He went on, even as I wondered at the candid admission. Did he suspect that Gretchen had already given me the details?

"You know, aside from its history and the fact that it's so beautiful, the Sunrise fascinates me because — well, it's something that's absolutely one of a kind. I've been hung up on that sort of thing for as long as I can remember. Even when I was little and the other guys were collecting the usual stuff, baseball cards and comic books or model airplanes, I'd save my money till I could buy something different, something special."

Abruptly, he reached for my hand and held it between his, one finger pressed gently against the pulse point at my wrist. "And speaking of something special," he said in a quick change that stunned me, "it's what I thought the first minute I saw you. Was that three years ago? No, closer to four. And even then you were such a beautiful little kid, I used to watch you and think — wow — when you grew up a little more —"

He added reproachfully, "Back then you couldn't see anybody but Hunter. I knew I didn't have a chance. But you've grown up a lot since then. Hard to tell what's going on in your head. Do you still feel the same way about Hunt?"

"I — I never dreamed you — that you felt — that you —"

"Well, now you know." He leaned over and kissed me, a long, disturbing kiss. Corey was very good-looking. I suppose I responded to that totally unexpected kiss as any girl would. And all the while, I felt uncomfortably aware of his fingers on my racing pulse.

Just as he drew back, I heard Bonnie's voice behind us, purring softly, "Oh, I'm sorry. Am I interrupting anything?"

Corey said amiably, "Matter of fact, yes, you are. And you probably aren't half as sorry about that as I am."

I scrambled to my feet. "Time I started on those phone calls, anyway. Did you and Gretchen make a list of people who might have called her yesterday?"

"Yes." Bonnie plunked herself on the chaise lounge and smiled up at me. "I made about a dozen calls. Why don't you go up and let me take a break? You might even try to find out why it's so vital, tracing whoever it was — I mean, what difference does it make? Wouldn't they call back eventually if it were important?"

I muttered something and fled, hoping I hadn't looked as flustered as I felt. But undoubtedly those sharp green eyes had seen everything I tried to hide.

8

As it turned out, my poise had been so thoroughly shattered, I couldn't hide much from Gretchen, either. She knew me better than Bonnie did, of course.

The minute I went into her room, closing the door behind me, she looked up from the phone on her bedside table, then slowly replaced the receiver.

"What's the matter?"

I collapsed in the chair by her bed. "Oh, of all the dumb things. I went out to the rose garden and Corey was there. And — wow, talk about lousy timing — I just wanted to be by myself for a while so I could *think*. About everything that's been going on around here."

I took a deep breath, aware of her steady gaze. "And all of a sudden — we'd been talking about the Sunrise — Corey began talking about *me*, how he felt about me, I mean. Listen, I didn't have a *clue* that he was interested in me. And — while I was still in shock, you know? — he leaned over and kissed me. And who came along just in time to see us but the Gorgeous One."

Gretchen giggled. "I know you're not that fond of Bonnie. Maybe I'd feel the same way if I hadn't known her all my life. She's okay — as long as she doesn't feel threatened. So, if she just saw you kissing Corey —"

"I wasn't kissing Corey. He was kissing me."

"— she'll figure you aren't interested in Hunter, after all and —"

"I'm not kidding *anybody* about that," I said gloomily. "At least I didn't a couple years ago. Corey says he knew how I felt. Gretchen, was it that obvious?"

"No, of course it wasn't. And isn't. Not to Hunter, anyway. I confess I haven't been positive about the way you felt until this minute. I had my suspicions, though. You two are so right for each other."

"Sure," I said flatly. "He's been coming on to me every minute since he first saw me. Unfortunately, he has only one thing in mind. He couldn't persuade me not to come to the house party, so he's pressuring me to go home."

"He's worried about you." Gretchen's voice was soft. "Just sick about what someone tried to do to me, and frantic for fear something else may happen — to you."

Cautiously, she shifted position to sit on the edge of the bed, dangling her feet. "I'm going downstairs this afternoon. I don't care what anybody says. You let me know the minute that chair thing is working, okay?"

I nodded. "Gretchen? I'm curious, is Hunter trying to get Bonnie to leave, too? And Corey?"

She shrugged. "Beats me. I don't know how he actually feels about Bonnie. You have to admit, she's fantastic-looking. And she can be fun when she isn't zeroing in on some guy. Right now, she's after Hunt. I warned you about that.

"As far as Corey's concerned, maybe Hunt figures Bonnie'll give up on him eventually and take off after some other guy. With Peter already spoken for, and a hunk like Corey available. . . . Well, she simply isn't interested in him. If my idiot brother ever asked, I'd tell him as much. She likes Corey okay. Everybody does. But —" A pause.

She scowled fiercely, looking in that moment so much like her brother, I grinned to myself.

"I guess I should say everybody likes Corey — with one exception. And that's Hunter. Something happened way back when we were little kids. Hunter wouldn't ever talk about it. Still won't."

We sat in silence for a few seconds. I stared across the room at her dresser where a picture of me, aged fourteen, smiled back. Then Gretchen sighed and picked up a small leather book inscribed, in gold letters, *Phone Numbers*. "Guess we better get back to work."

She glanced at me. "I forgot to tell you about Bonnie's anonymous letter. She hid it in the pocket of a sweater hanging in the closet. But when she came up after breakfast to get it — gone. Whoever swiped yours — well, they got hers, too."

I nodded, hoping my face didn't reveal what I was thinking. If Bonnie herself had sent me that nasty little note, she might have tried to divert suspicion by claiming she'd received one, too. And if she'd searched my things yesterday, breaking the lock on my vanity case in the process — Gretchen was watching me, so I quickly detoured from that avenue of thought.

For well over an hour, we took turns making calls. At that point Gretchen had reached all but three of the friends she thought might have called her yesterday morning.

"Well, that's it," she said wearily. "All but three — and they're out of town. Not likely that they —" She ran her fingers through her hair. With her big eyes, she looked more than ever like an abandoned waif. "Thanks, Alex. And there's the lunch bell. You'd better go down."

"How about you?"

"I'm going to get dressed. Right now, I'm working up a good mad. If that chair thing isn't finished, I'll ask Peter to carry me."

But apparently, the work on the chair elevator had been completed. It stood in position at the bottom of the stairs. In confirmation, when I went through the French doors to the patio, I saw Grandpa Luther stumping across the lawn behind his chrome walker.

Alden followed, his eyes watchful. I laughed to myself at the expression on the old man's face. It looked a lot like a toddler's mischievous smile as he manages to keep just two steps ahead of the person chasing him.

Margaret had arranged a buffet on a long, wide table. Corey and Delphine and Kendall were already sitting nearby. Much to my relief, Corey merely waved and turned back to them. I certainly didn't feel like talking to him again, not this soon, anyway.

Delphine's head bobbed firmly as she made a point to her husband. Kendall nodded agreement, but I thought his handsome, austere face looked tired. As I watched, he leaned back and pinched the narrow base of his nose, a characteristic gesture.

A moment later, he glanced at the table nearby where Hunter and Peter and Niles had their heads close together in sober conversation. Kendall's expression changed abruptly from one of weary amiability to cold anger.

I caught my breath, shaken, as I realized the ugly emotion revealed in this off-guard moment was directed at Peter. What a shame, I thought, because Peter might be his son-in-law some day. If that happened, Kendall would lose his last chance for a close relationship with his daughter.

Caught for a minute or two in unhappy speculation, I stood watching Margaret cut lemon slices for the pitcher of iced tea. After she fixed a plate for Grandpa, I served myself and asked if I could sit with him.

"Honey, I'd like that," he said, pleased.

We were almost through eating when Hunter and Peter approached our table.

Peter's face was stiff with strain. "Sir," he said to Grandpa, "I'd like your advice about the best time to notify the police about my father's disappearance. With a description of the car, too, I suppose —"

The old man studied him, sadness in the faded blue eyes.

Before he could reply, Delphine spoke impatiently from the next table. "Really, Peter, I think you're being impulsive. If you tell the police, it'll be embarrassing when word gets out. And word always gets out. Something like this, why, the wire services would pick it up in a minute. They always watch for items about well-known people."

Peter's voice sounded coldly polite. "I've called my family, ma'am. There's been no word from my father. No explanation for —"

"Perhaps he wants to take care of this emergency — whatever it was — before he —"

"What emergency?" For a moment, anger flared in Peter's dark eyes.

Delphine made no attempt to conceal her annoyance. "I keep telling you," she said sharply. "You either aren't listening, Peter, or you don't believe me. And I can't think what reason I'd have to tell you something that isn't true."

She paused, dabbing at her lips with a napkin. "Shortly after you and your father arrived, he came to me to say he wanted to apologize beforehand — that's exactly what he said — because a "business emergency" might call him away. At any hour, he said. His precise words. To my mind, that clearly meant any hour of the day — or night."

A brief, tense silence.

When Peter did not respond, Delphine glanced

at Margaret. The housekeeper had paused in the act of filling Kendall's glass to listen to the exchange.

"Margaret, you were there. You heard what Mr. Braun said. For goodness sake, relieve this young man's mind. *Tell* him his father was called away by some business crisis. And there is nothing *sinister* about the way he left Meadowmount."

Margaret put the glass down and smoothed her apron. "That's right, Mr. Peter. I heard your father say just what Mrs. von Weber's telling you. Some business emergency. And he said he was sorry about it. Seemed to feel it wouldn't be a proper thing to leave without a moment's notice, if it happened like that."

Peter's lips thinned. Then he muttered something and strode across the patio, Hunter behind him.

Beside me, I heard Grandpa say softly, "No, that's not the way of it. It wasn't that way at all —"

As I stared at him, he stiffened, his head came up, and for a moment, the old eyes blazed. "Gretchen!"

I turned to see her emerging from the living-room door. Bonnie had hold of one arm, and Gretchen leaned heavily on one of Grandpa's blackwood canes. It was not her presence that startled me, but the stormy brown eyes that froze the breath in my throat. I knew she must have heard what Delphine and Margaret had just told Peter.

Her voice emerged in a tone only a shade above

a whisper, yet it carried across the sudden silence. "Are you surprised that someone finds it hard to believe what he's told in this house? Don't you think it's about time we questioned the *simple explanation* for some of the things that are happening around here?"

Kendall leaped from his chair and hurried to her side. "What are you trying to do?" he said harshly. "Just what are you trying to do?"

"To get at the truth." She glared at him. "It's time to face the fact that something's happened to Peter's father and call the police, get some help. Do you want somebody else to be hurt, someone else to disappear like Mr. Braun did? What are you all waiting for?" Her voice rose, cutting sharply across the still, warm air.

"Gretchen, sweetheart —" Margaret took two steps, but the look on Gretchen's face stopped her. Tears gathered in the prominent blue eyes. Her hands worked nervously, making little pleats in her white apron.

The tense, accusing voice continued. "I'm tired of waiting for somebody to *do* something — if it wouldn't mean unfortunate publicity, of course." She took a deep breath. "Listen, you people. Bonnie and Alex and I have called everyone in San Diego County who might have made that phone call to me yesterday morning. We drew a blank. Do you know what that means? Somebody set a trap. They took my phone out of my room, and then someone in this house — or from outside — called and asked for me —"

"Stop it!" Her father grasped her shoulder. "You're hysterical!"

She shook off his hand, staggered, and would have fallen if Bonnie hadn't grabbed her.

"I think it's awfully interesting," Gretchen said unsteadily, "that you all find it so painful to listen to the truth. Well, hear this. My fall downstairs — that wasn't any accident. Someone rigged up a length of fishing line for me to trip over. And I want to find the rat who did it. Is that so much to ask?"

In the silence, Margaret gave a shuddering sob. "Oh, Gretchen," she moaned softly. "My little Gretchen!"

9

Grandpa Luther spoke firmly into the painful silence. "I would like to go up to my room. Alex, would you help me, please?"

"Of course."

We left them, looking like characters posed in a *tableau vivant,* avoiding each other's eyes. As I passed Gretchen's parents, it seemed to me that their faces were etched with fear for the first time.

Why had Kendall tried to silence Gretchen before she could reveal the truth about her fall down the stairs, a fall that might have been fatal? What was he trying to hide? Was it possible that Kendall knew who had set the trap? Had Kendall tried to protect him?

Or her, I thought, amending my image of the suspect. Delphine might be capable of a rotten trick like that, given a reason, one that devious mind of hers considered valid. At the moment, I couldn't come up with any likely motivation. Neither could I discount her stubborn chin or the other bulldog aspects of her personality.

Strange lady. But I suspected her husband might try to shield her from blame, even to the point of the extraordinary performance we had just witnessed.

Grandpa settled himself carefully in the chair fastened to the big banister. As its mechanism clicked and hummed, the chair moved slowly upward. I climbed the stairs beside him, holding the thin, frail hand he held out to me.

"I hope you don't mind me taking you away," he said as we neared the top. "I'm an old man. I've had more than enough lately of anger and conniving, of people trying to hurt each other." He shook his head. His wispy white hair lifted with the movement, then settled back on his pink scalp.

"I thought maybe it would be a good time to tape more stories for you. To take our minds off — what's going on downstairs." The chair stopped, and he looked up at me, his eyes bleak. "Will you stay with me awhile, Alex?"

"I'd love to hear more of your stories. The recorder's still in your room, isn't it?"

He nodded. As if he had made up his mind to something, he murmured, the words barely audible, "I'll tell you about Alaska. I'll tell you how it all began."

A few minutes later, I sat facing him, anticipating with a ripple of excitement the story about the gold that Luther von Weber and Herman Braun had found in Alaska.

Grandpa's eyes were almost hidden behind the tinted glasses he wore when light bothered him. "The *City of Seattle* was an old steam paddleboat that went the inside passage to Skagway," he began. "I remember one day it got pretty chilly in the open, and I went up to get warm around the big smokestacks. Found they were keeping husky dogs up there, and the poor brutes were seasick. Just lying there, sliding to the ends of their long leashes and back again with every motion of the boat."

He gave me a faint smile. "Did what I could for them. I like dogs. As it turned out, that's where I met Herman. He'd come up there whenever he got a break from the galley where he worked. They didn't treat him so good down there, the youngest man in the crew, green at the job. And not too long over here from Germany, so he still had problems with the language."

The quiet voice wove a pattern of words that gave me a vivid picture of the two young men. They must have been a far different breed from most of the rough, gold-hungry older men heading for the fields up north. Herman and Luther shared a love of adventure, but a certain innocence and idealism as well. They decided very quickly that they got on well together. From the moment the boat docked, they were a team.

"Had the time of our lives," Grandpa said with a chuckle, "gawking at all the sights. Did Gretchen ever tell you we were thrown out of Soapy Smith's famous saloon? They took a dim view of greenhorn kids who didn't drink or gamble."

He warmed to his story. "At Skagway, we drew plans for the boat we'd need to go down the White Horse, the rapids, then the Yukon River. Paid thirty dollars for surplus lumber, I recall. Then, to get ribs for the boat, we climbed the side of the mountain to cut little saplings already cured from a forest fire. The boat was twenty-one feet long, flat-bottomed with flaring sides. We caulked the cracks with oakum and pitch. Then we cut a young tree to use as a sweep.

"We finished on a Saturday night, and the papers came in from the States that day. The *Post Intelligence* had big news in the headline: ADMIRAL DEWEY CAPTURES MANILA. So we bought a thousand papers, hauled them over the pass on our backs, and took them downriver. Sold them for fifty cents apiece. That's how we made most of the money for our grubstake."

I took a deep breath, glad the recorder was faithfully capturing every word. Caught up in the colorful shifting scenes described in Grandpa's frail voice, I couldn't possibly have taken adequate notes. And I wanted to remember every detail in the story.

Hundreds of miles away, several decades in the past, I saw those two young men in the sturdy boat going downriver. I watched Indians standing on shore, holding up silvery fish that gleamed in the sunlight. They called out, "Shoog! Shoog!" which meant they wanted to trade their salmon for the white man's sugar.

"On the banks of Lovett's Creek, that's where we found our gold," Grandpa said at last. He leaned forward now, excitement in his voice. "We dug a hole, you understand. Wasn't like what you see on television, a shaft in the side of a mountain or panning from a stream.

"No, we dug a hole, six to eight feet wide, and we went down thirty, forty feet. Sound like a pretty big project to you? Well, it was. Took a lot of time, a lot of backbreaking work."

He smiled. "That Herman was a fine worker. He never quit. But you see, the gold meant something different to him than it did to most of the men up there. He didn't want it for himself. He wanted what it could do for his family, both the family in the old country that he brought over eventually, and the wife and children he hoped to have one day.

"See why we made a good team? Both of us had one foot planted in the present, one foot pointed toward the future. And maybe something else, a tremendous, completely unwarranted, mule-stubborn faith in ourselves."

He laughed with real amusement, reached for a glass of water, sipped, and replaced the glass, his hand steady.

"We had our failures, too, in the beginning. At one point, we hit what they call a live glacier. That's frozen water below the surface of the soil. Had to quit there. And I recall there was mostly clear ice in the next hole, black muck above and below.

"When we found the right spot, we used a pick to chip out all we could in a day, sending the muck up to the top in a bucket we rigged up. Then, before we quit in the evening, I'd yell to Herman to send down some wood, birch and birch bark. I'd build a fire, climb aboard that bucket — it was big and strong enough to bear my weight — and light the bark. Then I'd hold my breath till I got to the top, Herman hauling me up with a hand-operated winch. The fire would thaw the ground so we could dig some more the next day."

He paused, removing his glasses to polish them with his handkerchief. As he stared out the window, his eyes were full of the past. "Finally, we hit a vein and got our gold, nuggets mostly, more than either of us ever dreamed we'd see. But then, just as winter was coming on, I got sick. That was bad luck up in those parts. More men died in Alaska from sickness than anything else, you know. You get wet and cold, camping on the shore of a river. Pneumonia was always a danger. We'd heard the stories, how the Indians would come in the spring and find men in their tents, still rolled in their blankets. Gone to a place where all their gold couldn't help them."

A soft sound of regret.

"I begged Herman to leave me, even let on that I was angry with him. Called him every name from fool to raving lunatic. Seemed a pure waste, both of us dying there miles from the middle of nothing, after all we'd been through. Busting our backs, slogging through the days too tired to eat sometimes, fighting mosquitoes and a dozen other pesky kind of flies.

"We weren't much more than boys, either of us, but I didn't want him to see how scared I was.

Herman being older, he never let on how his belly turned to ice whenever he thought about getting caught in a bad storm on the way out."

I watched, holding my breath, as he sat for a moment in silence, gnarled fingers plucking at the ends of his bolo tie.

"He pulled me through," he said then, his voice soft. "Nursed me day after day, praying the weather would hold. It did."

I let out my breath in a sigh of relief, as if I hadn't known how the story ended. These details explained Luther's devotion to his friend. But I recalled Gretchen telling me about other incidents, and I knew there were omissions in Grandpa's narrative.

He had saved Herman's life, as well, on at least two occasions, once when water poured into the hole from a thawed pocket in that underground glacier he had mentioned. And again on their way back to the States, when two men tried to rob them of their gold.

The old voice went on, hushed now, uncertain. "Lately, I can't help but wonder," he said, "if there's such a thing as a curse on gold that's taken too easily, as we took the gold from Lovett's Creek."

"But you worked hard for it," I protested. "You nearly died. I'd say you earned it."

He made a weary gesture with one hand, as if brushing my words aside. "A fortune," he said. "Even nowadays, men work long, hard years for that amount of money. It was a kind of guilt that made me put so much of it in the Sunrise, something beautiful for a lovely lady. Seemed to make more sense than spending it on fancy houses or trips to Europe, things like that. I bought land, yes, and worked it for a living. This house is big, but it was made for plain people. At one time, hired hands used one whole wing here at Meadowmount."

He hesitated, then said forcefully, "The Sunrise has brought trouble to this house. Something's gone fearfully wrong because of this beautiful thing."

He put his hand into a pocket in the leather chair and withdrew a chamois bag. The Alaskan Sunrise spilled out of it, glittering in the light from the window, molding itself to his frail hands. Once more, I found myself entranced by the sight of the world-famous necklace. And it had been tucked away in the pocket of an old man's chair!

The artisans across the ocean who had made it were long dead, I mused, along with the secrets of their craft. Yet, surely they had endowed the Sunrise with a kind of magic. Light sparked from the jewels as the old man moved the strands through his fingers, a lyrically beautiful necklace even apart from its history or mystique.

"Oh, Grandpa Luther, it's — it's fabulous!"

He leaned closer to put it in my hands. Awed, I sat for a moment without moving, thinking absurdly that it felt much like any other necklace, the metal cool against my fingers. Somehow, it looked as if it might be warm to the touch, brought alive in a sense by the radiance of its beauty.

After a while I handed it back. "Thank you," I said softly.

He nodded, then turned his head as we heard a series of creaks and scraping sounds. They seemed to come from the paneled wall behind him.

I wondered if I'd imagined hearing faint voices, too, and a burst of laughter.

Grandpa glanced at me, then down at the necklace. "What am I to do with it?" he said. "How can I set things right in this house as long as the Sunrise is here?"

I stared at him helplessly, unable to give him an answer, aware that he didn't really expect one. Again I heard the puzzling creaks in the wall.

"What's that noise?" I asked.

"There's a dumbwaiter in the wall. We don't use it much anymore. It was for when — when my Caroline was ill." He sighed. "The shaft was never closed off. I just had them hang a picture over it. Why don't you go check, sweetheart? Maybe the panel's open."

I went to lift one corner of the large painting. Sure enough, the panel was half-open. I could hear voices from the kitchen clearly. One of the girls below spoke in rapid sibilant Spanish, and another replied with a squeal of laughter.

Then I heard Margaret's annoyed question. "Is all that noise necessary?" Her words were distinct, despite a hollow effect as if she spoke into a tunnel. Suddenly, all was quiet again.

Trust Margaret to restore order, I thought, amused, and slid the panel across the dumbwaiter shaft. Turning, I found Grandpa watching me.

"I guess there aren't ever any easy answers," he said, and his voice sounded tired.

I realized it had been too long a session for him.

Before I could say as much, he went on. "When you come up against something that could be handled in half a dozen ways, all of them ending in trouble for someone, why, you —"

He hesitated, then finished on a stronger note "— you do what you have to do. Every one of us has to pay the piper for something we've done that turned out wrong, even though we started out meaning no harm." He repeated softly, "Meaning no harm."

The pain in his voice brought tears to my eyes.

His fingers trembled as he replaced the Alaskan Sunrise in the pouch. "You should have seen her wearing it, my Caroline," he said. "The picture never did her justice, though it made her look like a queen. She was beautiful even without jewels and fine clothes. True beauty comes from inside. It shone behind her face like the light from a lamp, warm and soft." He nodded. "Like lamplight."

With a sigh, he held out the pouch to me. "The safe's open," he said, "behind that picture of the horses. That's a Charlie Russell painting, girl. He's a fellow could paint the West like it really was."

I put the pouch in the small wall safe and spun the dial as he instructed. Then I left him dozing in his big chair.

As I went down the corridor to my room, I wondered if Grandpa Luther made a habit of removing the Sunrise from the safe. If he did, I suspected the rest of the family might be unaware of it.

I saw the object on my bed the instant I entered the room. It was propped against the pillow close to the window, and the harsh afternoon light glanced off its glossy surface. It looked for a moment like the picture of a skull.

My heart thudded hard, painfully, as I walked to the bed, my steps reluctant. Then I felt a cold wave of revulsion as I saw what someone had left in this spot where I'd be sure to see it when I opened the door.

It was a photo of me, the one I had given to Gretchen years ago. I had seen it on her dresser just before I went down to lunch.

Now I felt sick as I stared at it. Someone had cut out the eyes in the picture and left a ragged, gaping hole where the mouth had been.

10 ▬

I soon realized there was little chance I could nap as I had intended. Stretched out on the bed, I tried to relax, but my nerves tightened each time I reviewed the latest ugly incident.

Someone in this house had acted with sick, single-minded purpose, to frighten me. Taking my picture from Gretchen's room, mutilating it and leaving it on my pillow for me to find — these were direct, deliberate acts, more threatening than an anonymous letter and far more frightening.

I had hidden the picture under the paper lining in the chest of drawers, handling it as gingerly as if it were contaminated from the touch of my unknown enemy. Of course the taint would be nothing more tangible than hatred.

Closing my eyes, I willed my body to relax, turning my thoughts aside each time they returned to the picture-message someone had sent to me. At last I went over Grandpa's story, replaying it in my mind just as he had told it.

Again, I felt a strong emotional response to the Alaskan Sunrise, a little thrill of excitement when I realized I had actually handled one of the priceless art treasures of this century.

When someone tapped on the door, it startled me so, my heart banged against my rib cage. I sat up, abruptly aware that my room was far away from anyone in the next wing or downstairs. Grandpa must be the only person anywhere near — and Grandpa usually turned his hearing aid off when he settled back for a nap.

Much to my relief, when I opened the door I saw Hunter standing in the hall, arms crossed across his chest. His face was tight with mingled impatience and anger, an expression I could understand.

The events at Meadowmount had escalated out of his control. I felt sure he must be ready to explode with frustration. I suspected, too, that he was almost as scared as I was.

"Come for a ride with me, Alex?"

Surprised, I hesitated for a moment before I nodded and followed him down the corridor. Neither of us said anything until we got into his car.

Then he leaned toward me with a look in his dark eyes that made my breath catch in my throat.

"I want to talk to you. But you always get so uptight. Can we just have a reasonable discussion without — I don't want to fight with you, Alex."

"Terrific." My voice was cool. "We won't fight if you'll stop telling me to go home. Both Grandpa and Gretchen have asked me to stay, Hunter. I know you want me to leave, but —"

He made a soft, exasperated sound. Then he started the motor, and he didn't speak again until the car rounded the curve onto the blacktop road at the boundary of the von Weber property.

"You may not believe it, Alex, but the only reason I want you to leave is because I'm concerned about you. I don't think either Grandpa or Gretchen knows the whole story about what's going on at Meadowmount. Nobody does — except the person who's making trouble. But Gretch is right about one thing. It's time we faced the truth."

He glanced at me. "Yeah, Bonnie filled me in on the hassle at lunch."

A perverse impulse made me ask, "Have you asked Bonnie to go home? Or Corey?"

"Bonnie's sure Gretch is just imagining things. I figure it may be wise to let her go on thinking that. Safer. Neither Gretch or Grandpa ever confide in her much. Not like they're doing with you, for some reason."

He didn't sound happy about that. After a moment, he added, "And Corey wouldn't leave, even if I asked him to. *Especially* if I asked him."

I puzzled over that as I studied his grim profile. His hands gripped the wheel in a beginning-driver position quite unlike his usual expert but casual control. It seemed to reveal a great deal about his state of mind.

"Someone in that house is *sick*," he said into the silence. "It's dangerous being around somebody you know is mentally disturbed, capable of violence. But bad as that is, there's something a whole lot worse. Being around someone who's got a real problem — when you *aren't* aware of it."

He scowled at me. "Grandpa knows more than he's letting on, and he's in bad shape worrying about it. Not good at his age, tearing himself apart."

His voice sounded harsh. "And look what happened to Gretch. Maybe she's lucky to be alive. Might have broken her neck in a fall like that. It's hard to believe somebody in the house is responsible, for whatever reason. I guess it must make a twisted kind of sense to someone with that kind of bent brain —"

Again, I heard Grandpa Luther say in my mind, " . . . pay the piper for something we've done that turned out wrong, even though we started out meaning no harm. . . ."

We? Who did he mean? And if he had suspicions about someone in the household, perhaps that person knew it. Wouldn't that mean that Grandpa was in danger, too?

I shivered. My voice sounded uncertain. "You're positive then that nobody outside the house had anything to do with — well, with Gretchen's fall, for one thing? How about the phone call?"

"Could have been made from inside the house," Hunter said. "There must be eight different phones in the place, with a jack in nearly every room. When Grandma was ill, Grandpa had all the extra equipment put in so there wouldn't be a minute wasted calling for help if she needed it. Anybody could have called in from the gatehouse, too, or the old stable on the other end of the property."

He stared ahead of him, guiding the car around the bends of the mountain road with the ease of long practice.

"To answer your other question, no, I don't think anybody outside the house is involved. Can't be sure, naturally, because I haven't a clue about anybody inside the house, either. But if I can't figure out a possible motive for anyone in the family, and I can't, there's even less reason for anybody outside Meadowmount to be doing these things."

I saw the tight line of his jaw and guessed he might be thinking about Corey. I decided to ask him, directly. Then I had to be honest and add, "He seems to be up front about everything, as far as I can see. I don't know him as well as you do, of course, but —"

Hunter didn't answer. A moment later, he pulled off the road at a lookout point. We got out to enjoy the fabulous view of a good bit of the high country around us, distant peaks purple in the afternoon shadows and, thousands of feet below, the sweep of desert floor. It rolled for miles in a pattern of gold and brown, with an occasional square of green marking irrigated sections of small farms, miniature jigsaw pieces from this distance.

I recalled a time years ago when he explained with considerable amusement to Gretchen's little towheaded friend that this, the Sunrise Highway, had not been named for the Alaskan Sunrise, nor did it have any connection with that remarkable piece of jewelry.

"I suppose this road got its name because you can see the sun rise from down there on the desert when you're up here," he said. "Grandpa says there's one place along here where water that flows on the west side would go to the Pacific, and on the east, to the Gulf of Mexico."

Now he pointed out the old stagecoach route, and I tried to visualize horses and a tiny coach winding through the valley below, a plume of dust behind it.

The wind blew in our faces, hot and dry as the sandy expanse it had crossed. It made my eyes feel scratchy and my skin tight and stretched, as if every bit of moisture had been sucked from it.

Santa Ana winds, they call them in southern California. I once read that this is a corruption of the old Spanish word *satana*, meaning devil.

Devil winds. I turned away from the hot blast in my face, agreeing again with the name connecting these winds with an even hotter climate. In this part of the country, they are feared, as well, because they create a fire hazard. Here in the mountains, as Hunter had told me on the ride up, the brush was heavier than usual from spring rains, and now it was tinder-dry.

In the car, Hunter squinted at the hillside down the road. "A Santa Ana is all we need," he said darkly. "This whole area could go up like a bomb. One dumb driver flipping his cigarette out the window, and a strong wind like this to get the blaze going real good, and —"

I heard the worry in his voice. "Would Meadowmount be in danger?"

He shrugged. "We've had fires come close a time or two. The house is safe. Most of the land around it is cleared far enough back, so there's not much danger. We'd lose stock, though, and fences and outbuildings. Thing is, with a fire just over the hill, it's no picnic riding it out. When you're in an old house like Meadowmount, there isn't air conditioning to filter the junk out of the air. If it happens to be as hot as it is today, it's no fun at all."

He started the motor. "If you're going to stay around, better keep your fingers crossed. Once a big one gets started, you'll be stuck up here. They close the roads to everything but fire equipment." He added a little reluctantly, "Well, I have to admit, we don't get the real barn-burners very often."

We rode in silence for several minutes. I saw a few horseback riders and a crowd of kids cavorting in an outside pool in front of a trailer park. But not many people were outside in the heat at this time of day. In the sparse traffic, I noticed an unusual number of rangers in trucks patrolling the area.

Hunter went back then to the subject of the trouble at Meadowmount, perhaps to get our minds off another very real danger, the possibility of a bad fire nearby.

In any event, he picked up the thread of our conversation as if twenty minutes had not intervened. "Corey is open about himself only when it suits him, Alex. You should know that by now. He's an expert when it comes to rationalizing what he does."

Takes one to know one, I thought, annoyed by his tone. Even if he were right about Corey, and I had serious doubts that he was, why would he assume I knew Corey that well? He never talked a great deal about himself. It was one of the things I liked about him. Despite his fantastic good looks, he seemed to have only a normal amount of ego.

"You certainly don't think Corey set up Gretchen's accident," I said. "What possible reason — ?"

"What reason would anyone have?" Hunter shot back, his voice sharp. "Grandpa obviously thinks the Sunrise is behind everything that's happening. Hasn't he told you that?"

I nodded.

"Well, doesn't it make a difference, if you study the problem from that angle? Somehow, setting Gretchen up has something to do with someone's plans for the Sunrise. No, I can't explain how or why, either, but I don't know everything that Grandpa does."

I thought for a moment. "But why are you hinting out loud that something's wrong about Corey?"

"What's so right about him?" he said crossly. "Why do people assume you have to be crazy about somebody you grew up with? If you disliked someone when you were little, chances are that isn't going to change over the years."

I looked at him, remembering what Gretchen had told me, and wondered what had happened between Hunter and Corey when they were children. "Look, just because he'd like to see his father get some kind of insurance deal on the Sunrise —"

"It isn't that."

"— and maybe he has a sort of obsession about one-of-a-kind things —"

Hunter snorted. "That's just the reason he gives people for — for some of the things he does." He went on, thoughtfully, "I'll tell you something about Corey, Alex, even at the risk of having you think I'm putting him down because of the way he feels about you. I'm going to tell you, anyway. I want you to be cautious — even suspicious — of every single person at Meadowmount — *everybody* — until we find out who's responsible for the things that are happening."

He pulled off the road again, this time to bump along a rutted lane for several minutes, until it emerged into a small clearing. A sign posted on a nearby tree read, *Round Peak Plantation, Cali-*

fornia Agricultural Service. Beyond, I could see rows of small pine trees extending to the edge where I knew there must be a sharp drop.

Hunter led me over to a stream fed by an underground spring that spilled down the rocks in a small waterfall. The sound of the water splashing into the pool below gave the illusion of coolness. Perched on the grassy bank, I took off my sandals and dangled my feet in water that was almost too cold to bear.

In my mind, Hunter's voice said over and over, ". . . *having you think I'm putting him down because of the way he feels about you . . . because of the way he feels about you. . . .*" Did it mean Hunter cared — even a little bit — how Corey felt about me? My heart thudded so fast for a moment, I panicked for fear Hunter might hear it.

Beside me, he said slowly, "When we were little, we all had a lot of animals. In this area, we could get just about anything we wanted. I remember a boy on the Miller ranch had a wolf cub so tame, it followed him like a dog. And some of the guys had trained falcons."

He scowled at his hands clasped around one knee. "I never wanted anything like that, something that preyed on small animals. And I hated to see anything caged, especially an animal taken from the wild. So my own favorite was a baby raccoon. Niles found it after its mother had been killed, and he brought it home to me. I named him Rufus, raised him on a bottle.

"Lingo was the youngest of the dogs then, just

in training. Niles taught them to ignore Rufus, so he could have the run of the place. They say raccoons turn mean when they reach full maturity. Probably it's best to retrain them so they can be released in the wild again."

He paused. "Never had the chance to make that decision. Three months after I got Rufus, somebody gave Corey a baby coon, older than Rufus but still young enough to adjust well. So then there were two of us with an unusual animal."

He looked at me, anger smouldering in his eyes. "Corey has a 'sort of obsession about one-of-a-kind things,' all right." His sardonic voice put the phrase in quotes. "A short time later, he was the only one with a pet raccoon."

My mouth went dry. I swallowed with difficulty. "What happened to Rufus?"

"Someone left the back gate open. It isn't there anymore. Grandpa replaced the old fence with the block wall."

I said at last, "But — the open gate — anyone could have left it open. Accidentally."

Hunter shook his head. "I found a trail leading into the woods. Shells from fresh shrimp. Rufus would have gone to the moon for something like that. Why would anybody but Corey be interested in luring my raccoon through that gate?"

"Did you ever accuse him of it?"

"What good would that do? He knew he'd done it, and he was well aware that I knew it, too."

I stared at him. "You should have given him

a chance to explain, Hunter. Maybe you were mistaken."

He gave a short laugh. "Not likely. But maybe it was a mistake to tell you all this. I thought — well, I figured you for the kind of girl who'd be sharp enough to see through somebody like Corey."

"Thanks a lot. Looks like you wasted your vote of confidence, huh?"

He got to his feet and scowled down at me. "Can't talk to you for ten minutes without getting into some kind of hassle. Okay. You want it spelled out? I don't give a damn whether or not you think I'm wrong about that clown. I leveled with you for just one reason. Your own protection."

Furious, I scrambled to my feet, ignoring his outstretched hand. "If you'd stop treating me like a ten-year-old, maybe we'd get along better. There is no way you can convince me I need protection against — against Corey Atkinson! That's — it's the craziest thing I've ever —"

"Okay, forget it," he snapped. "I might have known you wouldn't listen. But if you're smart, you'll listen to me and be on guard against everybody at Meadowmount. You may not believe anything I've told you. That's your privilege. But you know Corey has a hang-up about one-of-a-kind things. All I've done is fill you in about something else he goes after. One-of-a-kind things when they happen to belong to me. Things I think a lot of —"

He glared at me. "For some reason, he's got it in his head that you're someone really special to me. First, he tried to move in on Gretchen — even Grandpa — and now he's zeroing in on you. I thought you should know that."

He turned, took three steps toward the car, and flung the last words over his shoulder. "There's no way I'm going to do you any more favors, trying to warn you. If you get in trouble, it's your own damn fault!"

11

A Santa Ana condition always has a bad af-
fect on me. The tension during that silent
drive back to Meadowmount didn't help. By the
time I opened the door to my room, I had stopped
shaking with anger. But my gaze went immediately to the bed, and I felt a vast relief to see
nothing else had been left on the pillow for me
to find.

I hoped Gretchen wouldn't notice that the picture was missing. No point in upsetting her with
the details of still another dirty trick. I might
have told Hunter if he hadn't behaved like a complete idiot. At the moment, I didn't feel like talking to him about anything at all, ever again.

By the time I went downstairs that evening, my
gloomy thoughts together with the ceaseless
sound of the wind had made me restless and ir-

ritable. It seemed difficult to breathe in the smothering dry heat.

As I entered the big room to join the family, I saw Bonnie and Hunter on a corner couch, heads close together. Good, I thought wearily. The way I felt about him right then, I hoped she'd monopolize him all evening.

Corey came to my rescue with something tall and cool to drink, and I let him steer me to an old-fashioned love seat. Across the room, the rest of the household hovered around the little bar, Niles and Delphine and Kendall, Gretchen and Peter looking subdued and entirely involved with each other.

My head began to pound, a misery I can usually hide behind a vague smile. In this case, I had to cope with added stress — ding-a-ling Delphine cheerfully quoting statistics about the rise in the crime rate during a Santa Ana.

In her long yellow dress, she looked great, obviously a person who would thrive in the midst of the Sahara. She rattled on and on with an incredible fund of information about odd and irrational behavior caused by the weather disturbances peculiar to this area.

It was insensitive of her, to say the least, after the explosive scene at lunch. Delphine might be expected to blithely ignore the conflicts within the family, and to expect everyone else to do the same. But now she seemed to be slyly suggesting that Gretchen's outburst was nothing serious, merely the result of oppressive heat.

If I could have come up with a better excuse than a headache — that always sounds so phony — I would have skipped dinner. Trapped within the range of Delphine's voice, I sipped my fruit punch. And winced inwardly at her mind-boggling rendition of facts and figures of interest only to dedicated weather analysts. And perhaps those weird people who collect trivia.

Then I saw that she was watching me, blue eyes thoughtful, and I gave her a polite smile that strained every muscle in my face.

At that precise moment, Corey said to me in an undertone, "Does your head ache, Alex?"

I looked at him, startled. "There's a crack in it right down the middle, but I thought I'd combed my hair so it didn't show."

"Everything shows in your eyes." He studied me, his head a little to one side. Then he lifted his glass. "You're a girl who smiles a lot. Sometimes that's a cover for — well, it could be a lot of things. Pain, shyness, maybe just a very private personality. But you don't play games. So when your eyes don't smile along with the rest of your face, I figure the only thing you're hiding is something like a headache."

At the end of the room, Bonnie laughed, a soft, silvery sound, and Hunter grinned at her, a wicked gleam in his eyes. She looked delectable in a lime dress, backless and with practically no front to it, either.

For a moment, I felt like an orphaned waif in my dumb pink blouse and pleated skirt. Silk and a yummy color, but a country mile from Bonnie's designer outfit.

I concentrated hard on the things that Corey had just said, trying to forget that fantastically pretty female — and Hunter's obvious appreciation. After all, the guy beside me had just offered the warm sympathy that I needed at the moment and perception I had never suspected.

More than I deserved, I thought with a twinge. Corey had been stuck with a classic also-ran tonight. Nobody special. Not in Hunter von Weber's opinion, anyway. A few hours ago, he'd made that very clear.

"Where did you learn so much about people?" I asked, and this time my smile didn't hurt a bit.

His clear gray eyes were quite serious. "Oh, I guess you pick up a lot if you're interested. Like the things people hide and how they manage to do it. And why."

He lowered his voice. "Take our hostess. You'd like to take her — for something like a one-way ride, if I'm reading you right."

He saw my expression and laughed. "Point is, I'm willing to bet nobody in this house knows what makes Delphine tick. Maybe she doesn't know, herself. Look, if you'd spent your whole life acting out various roles, doing what you thought was right, the things you figured were expected of you — wouldn't you be apt to wake up one day and realize you'd lost the person you were to begin with?"

"It's possible." I added, intrigued, "Well, if

you think that's happened to Delphine, what do you suppose she was like at the beginning? Before she got buried under all the parts she plays? There's the Model Wife, the Tolerant Stepmother, the Flaky Lady burbling malaprops — and the whoever-she-is right now, spouting statistics like a computer." I groaned. "Just our luck catching her act tonight when she's trying to make a point. I think I like her better flaky."

Corey grinned. "Yeah, but I've got a hunch that's not the real Delphine, either. And it's anybody's guess who that is."

"Okay, I'll let you go first. Guess."

He gestured at the big cabinet beside our love seat. "There's a clue right there. Everybody wonders about that collection."

The crystal miniatures. Of course. I'd wondered about them myself. Why was Delphine so fascinated with those tiny, fragile pieces of glass?

"No, her collection doesn't fit," I said. "Not any of the roles that I've seen. And there must be a half-dozen I didn't even mention. The Lady of the Manor, the Total Athlete. . . ."

Corey nodded. He finished his punch, glanced at my glass, and raised his eyebrows. When I shook my head, he leaned back, one arm across the back of the love seat.

"The way I figure it," he said, "it's a case of a lady who's always been a *big* person. Physically, I mean. When she was a kid, maybe even bigger than the boys in her classes.

"Only one way to go for somebody who needs

strokes. You set out to excel in things where height and weight and bones and muscles — they're all assets. They helped her win races and games and prizes and trophies."

He paused, glancing at me with a half-smile. "Those trophies, where do you suppose *they* are? How come they aren't on display instead of all the little crystal figures?"

"Beats me."

"Maybe because medals and trophies remind her of the way the kids teased her when she was the fourth grade klutz. Every time she looks at them, she remembers why she went after prizes in the first place. Because she couldn't win what she really wanted. Friends."

I stared at him, uncomfortable now. Was he still playing our silly game, analysis for a nickel? Or had he been telling me things told to him in confidence, perhaps by Delphine herself?

Years ago, I used to wonder why Gretchen had never been interested in Corey as anything but a casual friend, despite his extraordinary good looks. Eventually I realized the answer might be simply because Delphine was fond of him. Maybe she'd even been foolish enough to suggest that Corey would be a far more suitable boyfriend than Peter Braun.

As usual, I went the direct route and asked the questions I couldn't answer. "Corey, are you still guessing about — the things that happened to Delphine? Or did somebody tell you all that stuff? And if they did, how come you're telling me?"

He gave a startled laugh. "You never mouse around a subject, do you? Wow. Right between the eyes."

He leaned closer then, clearly taking no chances on anyone overhearing what he was about to say, though nobody seemed to be paying any attention to us. Kendall and Delphine and Niles were still at the bar, deep in sober conversation. Gretchen and Peter had walked slowly down the long room and through the French doors into the rose garden. Hunter and Bonnie remained on the couch, talking quietly.

"I'm guessing, of course," Corey said, "but I'd be willing to bet I'm right. Inside that big, bumbling, broad-shouldered lady is this tiny, delicate, completely feminine person trying to get out. She can't. And nobody knows she's there. The way I figure, that's the reason everything Delphine does is — not quite what you expect. Sets your teeth on edge. And of course she still isn't winning any friends. I'm really sorry for people like that."

He took a deep breath. "Sure it's only my theory about her, but — you want to know why I'm telling you all this stuff." He studied me for a moment. "I don't know whether you're a good judge of people or not, Alex. That's — well, that's why I'm taking so long to get to the point. Appearances can be deceiving. Don't make up your mind about anybody till all the facts are in."

I stirred uneasily, aware of what he was asking. He wanted me to withhold judgment on *him*, despite what Hunter might have told me. He probably knew Hunter and I had been together this afternoon, and suspected that we'd talked about him.

I would have given a lot to know what was going on behind those candid gray eyes. Had Corey actually lured Rufus, Hunter's raccoon, into the woods? Had he been capable of a mean trick like that, merely to insure that he'd be the only kid in the area with an unusual pet?

I found it hard to believe. Anybody could have left that gate open. Besides, there might have been more than one person interested in getting rid of a household pet as mischievous as I'd always heard raccoons could be. Certainly, Delphine would have been less than fond of him. A word to Alden, and Rufus would disappear with no one the wiser.

Now, I said slowly, "I try not to make snap judgments about anyone, Corey. I've been wrong too often to trust first impressions."

He nodded and left it at that. At dinner, we talked mostly about our plans for college.

"Gretchen says you've got some kind of job," he said. "Anything interesting?"

"No. I just wait on table in a little family restaurant whenever they need extra help. Only job I could find. Most places give priority to college kids. And that makes it rough for people like me, trying to save up enough money to get through the first year."

I shrugged and changed the subject. Corey

might be a whiz at instant analyses of people he'd known most of his life. But he was still a rich kid. What would he know about money problems?

Even Gretchen had asked if my job was fun. Did I make a fortune in tips? I laughed and said no to both questions. That's why I wanted to go to college, so I'd never have to wait on tables, ever again. She looked a little puzzled and told me firmly to quit the dumb job, that I was meant for better things.

After dinner, I escaped to my room with a great deal to think about. I showered and curled up in the chair to ponder Corey's theory about Delphine. The wind had died down a little, but the night air was no cooler. Still, my headache had gone except for a slight heaviness over my eyes.

"... *inside that big, bumbling, broad-shouldered lady is this tiny, delicate, completely feminine person trying to get out. . . .*" True? Possibly. But I couldn't go along with that as the reason for the absence of friends in Delphine's life.

I've often noticed a kind of reverse law when it comes to the ability to form successful relationships. Some people work so desperately hard to make friends that they end up driving all prospects away. And there always seem to be a fortunate few, like Gretchen, who attract everyone they meet with no effort whatsoever.

I decided to try to keep an open mind about Delphine. She would never be one of my favorite people, but that was because of her personality, mainly the lack of warmth.

Hunter had warned me to be wary of everyone at Meadowmount. Probably good advice, but I couldn't suspect Delphine of setting the trap that had hurt Gretchen. I got into bed at last, still silently arguing the point. For one thing, she would never consider behavior that other people might deplore.

Hours later, I woke from a confused dream in which Delphine sat at the dinner table with everyone watching her as she denied having anything to do with Gretchen's accident.

"She fell down the stairs," Delphine said in a disapproving voice. "It's the sort of thing that isn't done, you know. No one in the von Weber family has ever fallen downstairs —"

Everyone applauded, and the dogs outside began to bark.

I opened my eyes to see the room bright with moonlight. Outside, the dogs were barking in short, excited bursts. It sounded like the yapping of coyotes I often heard in the distance on warm summer nights.

I pulled the sheet over me and went back to sleep, thinking with a twinge of compassion that Soldier and Lingo must have cornered a rabbit.

12

The next time I woke, sunshine was pouring through the window. The hot wind still blew, no cooler even at this early hour. For a moment, I thought I smelled smoke, as if someone were burning leaves. *Must be my imagination,* I thought. No one would be burning anything with the strict fire laws in effect.

I listened to a mockingbird singing in the pepper tree just outside my window. Then, though the connecting door to the bathroom was closed, I heard voices in Gretchen's room, an urgent sound to them that brought me wide awake.

"All right!" Gretchen's words were high-pitched and angry. "I heard you. Now, please get out of here so I can get dressed."

A rumbling male voice made an inaudible comment. Her father?

"Wake Alex up? You've got to be kidding."

Gretchen again. "Who could sleep through all this yelling and hollering? No, I won't lower my voice. It takes a lot to light my fuse. But when it's burning good, stand by. If everybody in San Diego County finds out how I feel, that's just fine with me."

A door slammed.

I blinked and sat up. When the connecting door burst open, I pulled the sheet up until I saw that Gretchen was alone. "What in the world — ?"

"Good morning," she said in a voice that indicated it was anything but good.

Still in her robe, she clutched her clothes in one hand. Her face looked flushed, lips tight with barely controlled rage. Limping to the chair, she shrugged out of her robe and reached for her bra.

"Want some help?" I couldn't watch her clumsy movements without offering assistance, though I knew she'd refuse it.

"I can manage." It sounded as if her teeth were clenched.

Dressed at last in a white blouse and shorts and huge fuzzy slippers, she sat down in the chair, panting slightly, and glared at me.

"Thanks just the same," she said absurdly, several seconds after it no longer mattered. "Well, it's happened."

"What's happened?"

"Someone's made off with the Sunrise."

"What?"

She blinked, focusing on me as if she were really seeing me for the first time. "Niles just found the dogs. Drugged. Bones scattered around. Somebody fed them some doped-up meat. That same somebody must have gotten in the house after the dogs were taken care of. A few minutes ago, Daddy came roaring up to Grandpa's room and — the Sunrise was gone."

I stared at her. "He's all right?" I said at last. "Grandpa? He's all right?"

Gretchen gave me a faint smile. "That's my girl. Watch those priorities. Sure. He's fine. Slept through everything. But then, once he turns off his hearing aid, he'd sleep through the earthquake that's supposed to knock California off the map."

I sighed, relieved. "Is he — is he awfully upset?"

"Yes." She paused and frowned. "But I'm not reading him as well as usual. You know? It's as if he's — he's not as shook about the Sunrise being stolen as he is about — well, the way Dad's handling things."

She shook her head, as if her own words had triggered something else. "I'm not what you'd call one bit cool or objective at this point, either. Might as well give it to you straight, Alex —"

She looked at me, dark eyes burning with the emotion that hardened her voice. "Dad's making a big thing of the fact that you were the last one to handle the Sunrise."

My mouth opened, but my voice deserted me. I felt my face grow hot. Then, for a moment, I assumed the role of a dispassionate observer and thought how guilty I must look.

"Well, that's why Grandpa's upset," I said, my voice a little unsteady. "He asked me to put the Sunrise back in the safe for him yesterday. So he'd feel responsible. Might even think it's his fault that I'm in a" — I laughed, and that sounded a little shaky, too "— an awkward position. Am I?"

"If you are, I'm on the spot with you." Gretchen lifted her chin. "More responsible than Grandpa, to boot. I'm the one who asked you to come for a visit. To help me figure out what's going on around here."

I groaned. "A fat lot of good I've been. Somebody set you up for a fall that could have been — a whole lot worse. Then Peter's father disappeared, and now the Sunrise is gone. And in between stuff like that, somebody keeps trying to get me to leave. And I can't think why. I'm such a flop as a girl detective, I haven't even been able to find out who's that anxious to get rid of me."

I felt a small chill on the back of my neck and regretted my choice of words. The mutilated picture of me came vividly to mind, gaping holes where the eyes and mouth had been.

Gretchen's voice was firm. "Don't worry about anything Dad says. He isn't making much sense right now." She added wearily, "As if we didn't have enough to worry about, now there's a fire. They think the wind knocked down a power line. Over thirty acres burned already. It's heading for the next ridge."

So I *had* detected smoke in the air. While Gretchen went on talking, I scrambled into my clothes, a sleeveless blouse, shorts, and sandals. "I'd better call Mom," I said. "If it's been on the news about a fire nearby, she'll worry."

Gretchen nodded. "You can call from my

phone. Tell her there's no danger. We've ridden out a lot of fires at Meadowmount." She hesitated, then added awkwardly, "Uh — don't mention — the Sunrise. Okay?" She rolled her eyes.

I knew she must be thinking of her father's reaction, should word get out about the theft of the famous necklace. After I'd made my phone call, reassuring Mom about the fire, I stopped off in the bathroom to wash my face. And scrub my teeth with extra care, because I'd lied through them about the great time we were all having at the house party.

A sudden thought struck me as I was brushing my hair, and I went back to share it with Gretchen. "The safe," I said. "You told me once, it was specially made, almost burglarproof. Well, I spun the dial like Grandpa told me. So how could anybody break into it without waking him? Waking the whole household, for that matter?"

Gretchen looked unhappy. Her voice sounded a little too casual as she dismissed the point. "Nobody broke into it. It was open. Maybe Grandpa opened it again and forgot."

Not likely, I thought and stared at her for several seconds, the hairbrush poised in midair. "Gretchen," I said then, quietly, "does Grandpa remember that I spun the dial after I closed the safe?"

Gretchen didn't answer for a moment. Then she got to her feet and limped to the door. "Let's not take anybody's word for it," she said, her voice tight. "Let's go ask him."

In the corridor, we found Peter leaning against

the wall, waiting for us. His smile was a pale imitation of the real thing, but he grasped my shoulder firmly. It was almost as if he'd said aloud, "I don't care what anybody says. I know you didn't have anything to do with the Sunrise, the way it's disappeared." At least I had Peter and Gretchen in my corner.

"We're going to talk to Grandpa," she told him in a tone that invited argument.

He shrugged and gave her a crooked grin. "Want to stand in line? Hunter and your father are in with him right now. Alden's waiting to give him his bath. And the law ought to be arriving any minute."

"Law? Oh." Clearly, Gretchen found it distasteful that someone would come to investigate the robbery. A large-scale investigation, I thought, more than a matter of the local sheriff asking everybody a lot of questions.

Today was Sunday, but I doubted if that would make much difference, with something like the Alaskan Sunrise involved. Eventually, word of the theft might be flashed from coast to coast, even overseas. People who had never seen the necklace, perhaps not even a picture of it, would still remark on its disappearance because they'd undoubtedly heard of it, of the romantic legend that surrounded it.

All of this went through my mind as we walked down the hall, Peter and I slowing our steps to match Gretchen's halting pace. I didn't realize what she intended to do until she stopped in front of Grandpa's door. With only a glance at Alden, sitting in a chair at one side, she reached for the doorknob.

"Gretch," Peter said. Then he sighed, resigned, and sat down on the floor next to Alden's chair, put his head back against the wall, and closed his eyes.

Gretchen stepped into the room, pulling me after her.

I closed the door and took a deep breath as Kendall and Hunter turned to stare at us. They did not look pleased by our intrusion.

Between them, Grandpa huddled in the big chair, looking at least a hundred years old and very frail. It was as if the events of the night had taken their toll by diminishing his small frame. The chrome walker stood in front of him, and a blue-veined hand stroked one of the handles. His fingers were trembling.

I looked away quickly before he saw that I had noticed. But when I looked back, he smiled at me, breaking my heart.

"Don't you fret, little Alex," he said, his voice thin. "There's been some trouble. And there's a misunderstanding about that trouble. But it has nothing to do with you, child."

Kendall stirred impatiently. For a moment his eyes met mine, and I felt the coldness in the man as if he'd touched me. It was not dislike that I recognized in that instant, merely a searching of my face by someone who hadn't the slightest interest in me. Not even the vague feeling of one human being for another — almost any other — on the entire planet.

"Grandfather's mistaken about that," he said. "The Alaskan Sunrise is gone, quite probably stolen by intruders who first drugged the dogs. But everyone — *everyone* — in the house must be considered involved in the theft until —"

As he paused, the old man said crossly, "We're all to be considered guilty until we can prove we're innocent. Is that it, Kendall?"

"Now, Grandpa, I don't think we have to include you on the list."

"Why not? I got the necklace out of the safe. And you're making it pretty clear that you won't take my word for it that this little girl put it back for me."

"On the contrary," Kendall said easily.

I could see Grandpa's temper rising at the conciliatory tone. His hand tightened around the handle of the walker. "Then take her name off your blasted list!" he snapped.

Hunter intervened. "If you could be sure that Alex spun the dial on the safe after you saw her put the Sunrise away —" He made a gesture of frustration. "I don't like this any better than you do, Grandpa. But we all know Alex is going to be questioned about everything that went on in this room yesterday afternoon. And that's one question they're going to ask."

"Should have fibbed about it," Grandpa muttered. "All this hullabaloo —"

Gretchen said a little desperately, "Grandpa, if you didn't see Alex spin the dial, maybe you heard it —"

"No," he said reluctantly. "I was so tuckered

out, I leaned my head back and closed my eyes and reached up —" His hand touched the bow of his glasses where the hearing aid had been built into the frame. "And then I went off the air," he said. "Pshaw! If I'd waited one more minute —"

"Well, you didn't, and it can't be helped," Hunter said briskly. "We'll have to work with what we have. Tell us, Alex, in as much detail as you can, everything you did while you were in here yesterday. Incidentally, how long was that?"

I glanced at Grandpa and surprised an odd, intent expression in the faded blue eyes. It was as if he were trying to tell me something. I looked away, my face carefully blank, though curiosity scratched at me. Did he want me to hold back some of the details Hunter had requested? And if so, which ones?

I would feel my way, I decided, reciting the facts slowly enough so the old man could cue me. I smiled at him and nodded slightly, trying to tell him, *Grandpa, I'm on your team.*

With no explanation, no answers at all, there was still no question in my mind that I'd do anything he wanted. And it would be the right thing for me to do.

"I came up here after lunch with Grandpa," I said to Hunter, as formally as if he were one of the detectives who would be questioning me. "He said he'd tell me more of the stories I've been taping for school. So I got the tape recorder going and —"

"Did you happen to check the time?" Kendall

asked. He stood on Grandpa's left, arms folded across his chest, watching me.

I'd seen Hunter assume the same posture a dozen times, but it had never irritated me as it did now. Somehow, Kendall made me feel as if I were already on trial for grand larceny.

"It was one-thirty," Grandpa said.

I swallowed hard. "I'm not sure how long he talked, but it'd be simple to check. It's all on the cassettes. A little over an hour, I guess. I stopped once to put on a new one."

"And then? When you finished and turned off the recorder?"

I didn't want to look at Hunter. The cool dark eyes would tell me again he'd warned me that I might get in trouble if I stayed around any longer. Besides, I wasn't anybody special as far as he was concerned. Sorry about that.

I didn't want to watch Grandpa, either. My expression might give me away if he did give me some kind of signal. I decided I'd have to tell it the way it happened and just glance at him from time to time.

"He showed me the Sunrise," I said. "He let me — he let me touch it, hold it in my hand."

"Did you get it out of the safe for him?"

"I got it out," the old man said sharply. "I had it when she started the tape recorder. After I got tired, she switched the machine off, and I showed the Sunrise to her. Then I asked her to put it back in the safe for me." He hesitated. "Then she went away, and I had a nap."

Hunter looked at me for what seemed like a very long time. I could feel my heart pounding slowly and deliberately as the seconds passed.

"You want to add anything to that?"

I turned to give Grandpa a direct look, as if I were considering the question carefully. Then I shook my head. "That's about it."

Kendall grunted. "You sat here?" He touched the back of the chair beside Grandpa. "You walked to the safe and you left the room — right away?"

"Yes." I looked at him, then at Hunter. Something flickered in those dark, impassive eyes.

"Okay," Gretchen said, louder than necessary. "Okay, that's it. Let's go down and get some breakfast before — before company arrives." She gave the words a wry emphasis.

I followed her out, waited until Peter had scrambled to his feet, and walked downstairs with him, Gretchen riding the chair elevator beside us. We didn't say a word. I haven't any idea what the two of them were thinking, but one question filled my mind.

Why hadn't Grandpa wanted me to mention that I had closed the panel of the dumbwaiter shaft?

13

Gretchen hobbled into the dining room, holding onto Peter's arm. She glanced at me as she sat down. "Forgot to tell you. I persuaded Bonnie to go home for a couple days. Nobody was in any mood for a house party — even before the latest, uh, happening. And both the guys seemed to think she'd be better off not knowing what's going on. So —"

Delphine and Niles paid no attention, attacking the food on their plates in a grim silence. As I settled in my chair, Margaret came in from the kitchen, looking tired and harrassed. Her lips tightened as she looked at Delphine, obviously the source of her annoyance.

Delphine erupted into speech, as if she'd been pondering her own problems and suddenly decided to air them. "Police! They'll be all over the place, trampling the rose garden, snooping into every nook and cranny. On a Sunday — can you believe it?"

I wondered if she'd find such behavior acceptable on a weekday. It was so much like the absurd scene in my dream that I grinned in spite of my gray mood.

Peter turned in time to catch my expression. He raised one eyebrow in a silent question.

I said softly. "She's talking just like she did in my dream last night. Then the dogs began to bark and I woke up — and they really were barking —" I broke off as I realized abruptly why they'd been so excited at that unusual hour.

I suspected Peter was thinking about that, too, because he merely nodded and said nothing.

Margaret spoke quickly to Gretchen. "I was going to come up and help you dress." She gave Delphine a bitter glance. "But I've been kept busy every minute since I got out of bed. Both Alden and Niles chasing around because of the fire. And I can't think what anybody expects the sheriff might find in my kitchen cupboards!"

Delphine's blue gaze was bland. "It's what we don't want the officers to find. Don't you understand, Margaret? Because of this dreadful thing, every angle of our privacy is about to be invaded!"

Peter choked on his orange juice.

I looked at him, expecting to see him politely disguising his amusement. But to my surprise, his black eyes sparked with anger. In fact, I was sure he would have made a sharp reply to Delphine's inanity if Hunter and Kendall had not come in just then to take their places at the table.

"I don't know what's gotten into him," Kendall exclaimed, his voice harsh. "Grandpa sleeps like a cat, one eye open, always has."

As he paused for breath, I glanced at Gretchen who had claimed Grandpa would sleep through an earthquake. But Gretchen sat staring at her plate.

"Claims he didn't hear a thing," Kendall went on. "Our prowler must have drugged the dogs, climbed over the wall, pried open a door, and then he came right in this house — !"

Niles's head jerked up. His colorless eyes glittered behind rimless glasses. "It wasn't any prowler who threw meat to the dogs," he said, and his voice, too, was edged in steel. "Soldier and Lingo have had years of training and discipline. They wouldn't eat anything thrown over the wall."

I drew in my breath. But Hunter asked the question still forming in my mind. "Are you saying — they knew the person who gave them that meat?"

"That's exactly what I'm saying." Niles sat, still glaring at Kendall. "And that's what I'll tell the police."

"They'll be men who know their business," Kendall snapped.

"Then they'll recognize the fact that I know mine." The caretaker was rigid with rage, plainly beyond caring how he spoke to the man who might one day be his employer. "It's my business to know my dogs. I've trained them to guard this property — and all the people who live here. If the sheriff's smart, he'll take my word for that. We're not looking for a sneak thief, a prowler — or anyone else outside this house."

Kendall slapped his napkin on the table, rocking the coffee in his cup. "Now just a minute, Niles! You take entirely too much upon yourself."

A moment later, his eyes wavered as they met the caretaker's stony gaze. Kendall looked away. When he spoke, the anger in his voice had been muted by a note of reason. "We're all still shaken up. Natural enough. Terrible thing. First, Walter Braun leaving the house under odd conditions, to put it mildly. And now the Sunrise —"

In his agitated state, he must have overlooked Peter's presence at the table. I winced inside as Peter straightened in the chair beside me.

His voice was very quiet. "I don't believe there's any connection between those two events," he said, "and I'm sure you don't mean to imply that there is."

Knowing Peter as I did, I knew that deadly tone should have warned Kendall to back off. Beyond him, Gretchen's small face froze with apprehension as she watched, her lips parted.

Kendall plunged on. Even as I listened, holding my breath, I thought, he'd never taken the time or trouble to get to know Peter. In a matter of seconds, he was going to regret that fact. "Implying a connection, am I? Look here, boy, how can anybody say at this point whether there's any connection — or not?"

A muscle jerked in Peter's jaw. *"Sir,"* he said, and the word was knife-sharp. "If you're going to insist on a possible connection, you're saying a lot more than you realize. I'll tell you what's *possible*. Maybe my father got in someone's way, someone

who valued the Sunrise more than the life of a —"
He said something in German, a long guttural
word or phrase.

We could only guess at the meaning. All but one
of us, that is. Behind me, I heard Margaret moan
softly, miserably.

Niles intervened once more, his voice cracking
through the silence. "Young man, just what are
you trying to say? And I'd thank you to say it in
English, if you don't mind." He rose from his
chair.

To my dismay, Peter stood up, too, and took
one step toward the foot of the table. It was un-
clear to me why Niles had taken offense at Peter's
remarks. I could be sure of only one thing in that
tense moment, the gratitude I felt when the door-
bell rang.

The sound effectively cut off a scene that might
otherwise have played to a disastrous conclusion.
Margaret hurried down the hall, returning a moment later with the sheriff and two men he introduced as detectives.

I couldn't help staring at the three men from a
world foreign to me. My only knowledge came
from police shows on TV. So I studied Sheriff
Hank Benbough with considerable interest, noting
his thin gray hair, blunt, florid bulldog face, and
his stocky body, the stomach a little soft under the
flashy western belt and oversize buckle. I decided
he'd look like a sheriff even without the uniform
he wore.

The detectives, on the other hand, bore no re-
semblance to their counterparts on the tube. They

looked more like shoe salesmen, the kind who work in factory outlets in a seedy part of town.

Both of them had tired faces, a drawn weariness around the eyes. They reminded me of a weird phrase my mother favors. I could almost hear her say it: "They look like they've been there and back a dozen times already."

Kendall bounced to his feet and hurried to greet them, obviously as relieved as the rest of us by the timing of their arrival. Tempers could cool now while the representatives of the law got their investigation moving.

As the four men went upstairs, Niles gave Peter one last hard look and strode from the room by way of the kitchen door.

Peter sat down, looking a little sheepish. "Sorry," he said. "Very uncool performance."

"Not at all." Hunter raised his juice glass in a salute, his eyes warm. "Pete, it's time to report your father missing. Before the sheriff leaves, we'll find out what the procedure is. Okay?"

Delphine started to say something. Then she glanced at Gretchen and subsided.

Gretchen eyed her for a moment. "Yes," she said, her voice firm.

The phone rang. Margaret answered in the kitchen, then came to plug a phone into the jack by the sideboard, placing it on the table beside Gretchen. "There, sweetheart. You don't have to move," she said.

The conversation was brief, but I think everyone at the table caught the gist of it before

Gretchen hung up, eyes wide as she stared at each of us in turn.

"Ann Castle," she said in a wondering voice. "She's been gone since Friday, but she says she called me just before she left. Margaret took the call, but — I never came on the line. Ann figured Margaret went off and forgot to call me. So she just hung up herself, eventually. And Bonnie didn't get hold of her till this morning, a half hour ago."

I leaned forward to look at her past Peter's shoulder. "So there *was* a call for you." I sorted my thoughts aloud. "And that means — well, how do we know now that the trap was rigged for you?"

"Don't forget," Peter said, "somebody took the phone from her room."

It's funny how things happen sometimes. Everyone's attention was on Peter for those few seconds. I had been looking at him, too, and glanced beyond at Delphine just in time to see a wave of color sweep from her throat to the roots of her hair. She picked up her napkin then and hid the flush of guilt behind it.

I took my time finishing my breakfast, even asking Margaret for coffee, which I don't really like. Luckily, Delphine seemed in no hurry to leave the table, either. As I sat searching for the right way to phrase my sudden suspicion, Hunter excused himself and went upstairs. A few minutes later, Peter and Gretchen headed toward the living room.

I had to ask my question twice. Delphine seemed

absorbed in her own thoughts for several seconds before her head came up and she looked at me, blue eyes startled.

"What did you say, Alex?"

I repeated quietly, "You were the one who took Gretchen's phone. Weren't you?"

She made an exasperated sound. "Everybody keeps harping on it!" She echoed the questions crossly. "Who made the phone call? Who took the phone out of Gretchen's room? Who planned it so she'd fall downstairs?"

A flick of her fingertips disposed of the past speculation. "It doesn't amount to a hill of pins," she said.

I didn't find her one bit amusing at that moment. "But — why? Why did you take her phone?"

"I tried to make a call three times that morning, and she was always on the line." Delphine's voice sounded grieved, defensive. "I finally went down the hall to ask her, *please,* to give me ten minutes. And she was in the bathroom, so I — I simply took her phone back with me. When I went downstairs a few minutes later, I simply forgot about it."

"But why didn't you say so before?"

Her eyes were wide with virtue. "I fully intended to say so, once everyone stopped being so emotional about it. Then when Gretchen talked so wildly at lunch yesterday, making terrible accusations, going on and on about somebody tying something across the stairs to — to make sure she'd fall —" She spread her hands. "Well, think what a dreadful position I was in."

After a moment, I sighed, unable to think of any reply that wouldn't deeply offend her. Delphine was simply one of those people on a different wavelength from everybody else. At last I just nodded and got up to go and join Peter and Gretchen.

I didn't get it all untangled until I was actually across the hall and halfway down that enormous living room. I stopped short then, jolted by the thing that had finally come clear to me. For a second or two, I stood beside Delphine's cabinet, staring at the delicate miniatures without seeing them.

I was vaguely aware that Peter and Gretchen had been arguing about something as I came into the room. Now they were silent, watching me. So I realized the terrible thing I was thinking must be reflected on my face.

It had hit me abruptly. If the trap had not been rigged for Gretchen, nor for Grandpa — unable to walk downstairs, usually carried down by Alden — that left only one other person upstairs just before lunch on Friday.

The intended victim must have been Peter's father.

14

"Alex?"

The urgent note in Peter's voice pulled me back to awareness. A chill slid down the back of my neck from the prickling roots of my hair. I thought, absurdly, *But it's such a hot day. . . .*

"Alex?" Peter said again. He held up a muttering transistor in one hand. "Were you listening to the news about the fire?"

I stared at him. "Fire? Oh. No, I wasn't."

"I thought Margaret might have brought in the radio from the kitchen. Your face —" He shrugged, not about to ask further questions, even if he had seen horror in my eyes. Peter was that way, always careful of intruding into someone's private space.

"It's burned several of the cottages down the road," Gretchen said, her small face pale. "Firestorms. Impossible to fight a fire very well in this wind. Gusts up to seventy miles an hour. Oh, if only the wind would stop."

"You mean — it's that close? It's already near the Tree Farm?" I had a painfully vivid picture of the area, the little stream by the rocks where Hunter and I had talked.

Peter nodded. "Fifteen of the summer homes gone. They got people out at two this morning. They won't save any of those homes unless the wind changes."

I shook my head. My mother would be frantic if she heard it on the news. But she did a lot of her shopping on Sunday. I hoped she wouldn't hear anything until after the fire was under control.

Somehow, the enormity of this new situation had less impact than the lightning bolt that had struck a few moments before. My mind returned to explore the bleak, newborn theory. If Peter's father had indeed been the intended victim of one trap, then Grandpa was right. Something had happened to him later. He had not escaped the second time.

For a moment, I seemed unable to move. It was as if the frantic activity in my mind had drained all my energy. I decided not to tell Gretchen and Peter that Delphine had taken Gretchen's phone. First, I wanted to compare notes with Grandpa.

Again, I felt a flutter of fear. There were too many things I didn't understand, too many people I couldn't trust, too many ways I could be in danger. I had to admit Hunter had been right about that.

I pushed the thought away, said something to

Gretchen about going up to my room, and went back to the hall. But just as I reached the stairs, Margaret called to me from the dining room.

"You're wanted on the phone, Miss Alex. Take it right there in the hall, why don't you?"

I picked up the phone in the alcove under the stairs, certain my mother had heard about the rapidly spreading fire, after all.

It was not my mother's voice I heard, however, but a hoarse whisper. "If you're smart, you'll put the Sunrise back in the safe. You have until ten o'clock tomorrow. Then go back where you belong. You could get hurt, playing games like this —"

I heard a click. But I retorted anyway, angry as well as scared, "Who is this? What are you talking about?"

Fumbling the receiver back in place, I ran to the kitchen. Margaret stood by the sink scrubbing an enormous skillet. She turned, startled, as I burst into the room.

"Margaret — that phone call — who was it?"

She gaped at me, white showing around her eyes. It made her look almost comically distraught. "How should I know who it was? I didn't ask. He asked for you and —"

"A man?"

A slight pause. "Well, of course it was a man," she said, her monotonous voice contrasting with the wild look in her protruding eyes.

"Did you ever hear the voice before?"

"No, can't say I ever did. Why — ?"

"Could it have come from inside the house?"

"Miss Alex," she said in the tone one would use with a very small child, "you weren't talking on the house phone. *This* is the house phone." A gesture at a small white phone on the wall. "I don't understand what you're getting at. What's wrong?"

I sighed. "I don't understand, either. It was somebody — a man — whispering, threatening me."

"*Threatening* you?"

"Somebody seems to think I'm the one who swiped the Sunrise."

"Ah," she said as if that explained everything. "A joke, no doubt. Mighty poor one, I'd say."

She wiped her flushed, steamy face on her apron, mumbling something about the Sunrise and idols of gold. "An evil day when that necklace came into this house. Even Mr. Luther says there's a curse on it."

"I don't think it was a joke," I said firmly, trying to get her back on the track.

She gave me a casual glance and shrugged, plainly dismissing the subject. With a scratch of annoyance, I realized that Margaret either didn't believe me or didn't care one way or another about the phone call. About to protest, I changed my mind. Maybe the housekeeper was concerned about so much, she simply had no capacity to worry about one more thing.

The house phone buzzed. Margaret wiped her hands and went to it. "Yes, sir," she said. "Yes, sir. Right away." She pressed a red button on the panel beneath the phone. After a moment, she spoke into it again. "Niles, you're wanted upstairs. Right away, Mr. Luther says." She listened for a moment. "I can't help that. He knows there's a fire, but he says —"

She hung up, gave me another distracted look, and made an obvious effort to pull herself together. "More coffee, Miss Alex?"

Alden came in the back door, nodded at me, and picked up the thermos on the counter. "Might make up something cold, too," he told his wife. "Got a crew working on the ridge. Tea would be good. Or lemonade. I'll be back for it."

Margaret watched through the window after the door closed behind him. Then she brought my coffee without comment.

"Thank you." I suffered a twinge of conscience. Didn't the poor woman have enough problems without adding one of mine to her burden? Still, I felt compelled to keep looking for answers.

"Margaret, Peter told me about your sister and her family," I said gently, watching her face. If it seemed too painful for her to discuss the matter, I'd drop it.

But she merely nodded and sighed. "It's hard to know what to do," she murmured. "You do what you have to do. But there's no denying, it'd be a sight easier to know — to be sure just where your duty lies."

"Margaret, did you have a chance to talk to Mr. Braun about it?"

She looked at me, her face blank. Then she brightened. "Mr. Braun? Why, yes, I did, Miss Alex. Such a kind gentleman. He said he'd be glad to try to check on the man. The *fluchthelfer*. You know. The one who got in touch with me about my sister."

She stared out the window for a moment. "You have to understand something about German families like Mr. Braun's. They have a — a discipline, a correctness that most Americans don't understand. Men raised in that kind of family — they don't do things in a hurry." She made a soft sound as if she didn't always admire the trait. "Well, when Mr. Braun returns home, I'm sure I'll hear from him. In time, I'll hear."

I sipped the coffee I didn't really want. "You still don't believe that — that something's happened to Mr. Braun?"

"Happened to him?" A puzzled frown. "Oh. You mean — foul play of some kind?" She said the melodramatic words with a straight face, entirely serious.

"No, Miss Alex, I can't go along with a notion like that. I heard him, you know, when he told Miss Delphine he might be called away. There isn't a bit of mystery about it, as far as I can see. His boy, well, he's making a fuss over nothing. I just don't think there's anything to worry about."

The phone rang, this time the one beside the white house phone. Margaret answered it, then beckoned to me, a glint of curiosity in her pale eyes.

The male voice on the line jolted me for a moment. Then I realized it was Corey. It would have been clever of him, I thought, if he had made the call ten minutes before, to call back now —

Horrified by the sudden unbidden thought — I was turning into a rotten, suspicious person — I put more enthusiasm into my greeting than I actually felt. "Hi, Corey. Missed you at breakfast." *What's wrong with me, anyway?* I thought with a twinge of guilt. I hadn't missed him at all.

"Came home to make sure our house wasn't in any danger," he said, sounding weary. "We'll be okay. But I've been up half the night helping on the fire line, and —" He broke off.

"But that isn't why I'm calling, Alex. I'm down at the ranger station. Guy here says the sheriff came by on his way out to Meadowmount. He had some crazy story about the dogs being drugged, somebody breaking in — what's going on over there?"

"Well, that's about all we know — except that somebody's going to climb the sheriff's frame if he doesn't quit blabbing everything *he* knows. He's talking to Grandpa Luther right now." I thought uneasily, and with another prickle of guilt, it might not be wise to tell him more even if I'd known anything else. Corey could have drugged the dogs as easily as anyone in the household. They knew him, too.

"Be there in a few minutes," he said at last.

I hung up and returned to my cooling coffee, marking time impatiently until I could go up and talk to Grandpa. The housekeeper seemed deep in her own brooding thoughts. I searched for something that might distract us. Not too surprisingly, the first thing that occurred to me concerned Corey in a way.

"Margaret, I went for a ride with Hunter yesterday." I saw from her slight smile that it was not news to her. "He told me about a pet he once had. A baby raccoon. He named it —"

"Rufus!" she exclaimed. "Oh, what a mischief he was, too. Can't say I was all that sorry to see the last of him, though I hated to see that little boy grieve. Nasty business, finding him like that. He loved the little creature."

"He found him?" I said, startled. "But I thought — he said the trail led to the woods, and — I guess I just assumed that he never saw Rufus again."

Margaret made a face. "I remember now, he made me promise not to tell. Didn't want Gretchen finding out. Well, it's years ago, not important anymore. Truth of it is, Rufus was poisoned. I never did know more than that. But I think Hunter did. From the look on his face, I had a notion he knew very well who'd poisoned his pet."

I went to stand with my elbows propped on the high sink drainboard, trying to get more details from her. But I realized eventually that she didn't know any more than she had told me.

It seemed hard to breathe the stifling air in the big kitchen. A sudden gust of wind rattled the windows, and something crashed against the back of the house.

Margaret swiped at the windowsill with a cloth and snorted as the black specks streaked along the surface. "Look at that. In my sink, too. I could wipe it up every five minutes and never get it all. Ash in the wind from the fire. More heat and misery headed our way. I'll get Alden to set up the big fans in the living room and hang wet towels in front of them." She clucked unhappily. "If that wind doesn't shift, it'll be worse before it gets better."

She turned on the kitchen radio. A few minutes later, the music stopped and the announcer cut in with the local news. It began with the fire report.

A Red Flag Alert, indicating extreme fire hazard, had been issued for the county twenty-four hours earlier. At that time, a task force of forestry rangers had been pressed into emergency service. Five companies of division fire fighters had flown into San Diego from Northern California stations to be deployed around the county.

Power lines tangled by winds gusting up to eighty miles an hour were blamed for the initial outbreak. A low humidity condition also harassed the fire fighters. Fifteen summer homes in the area, a country store, and several buildings connected to a campground were the first to be consumed by racing flames.

The announcer read the bulletin tensely, his voice somber. "Horse trailers carry animals from ranch corrals. A few hundred yards away, fire races along the canyon ridges — leaping from one patch of dry brush to another.

"Veteran ranger Joe Kenyan says this combination of dryness, heat, and high winds is the worst condition he's seen in thirty years of service. There is no sign of change. Local residents and fire fighters can only hope the Santa Ana winds will abate."

Side by side in front of the window over the sink, Margaret and I stared at the smudged sky over the ridge. My nerves tightened, repelled by the evil in a fire out of control. Yet, in that moment, I felt an equal pull of fascination and fear.

I left the kitchen just as Corey came in the front way and the men straggled downstairs, their faces closed and tense. Grandpa rode the chair elevator beside them.

I saw his stubborn expression, chin high, mouth firm, and felt my spirits lift. *He's in charge again, I thought. Things haven't been handled to his satisfaction, and he's begun to set them straight.*

Moments later, it was apparent that he'd done just that. At the foot of the stairs, he looked up at the sheriff. "Sorry you've been brought out for nothing, Hank. With this fire eating up the countryside, you're not going to have any trouble keeping busy today."

"Now, Grandpa," Kendall said, his voice sharp. "What do you mean, bringing him out for *nothing*."

Grandpa straightened his thin shoulders. For the first time, I heard a steely note in his voice. I suspected he reserved it for rare occasions when someone questioned his authority.

"I meant exactly what I said. There will be no investigation into the disappearance of the Sunrise."

"Disappearance!"

"You heard me." Grandpa's mouth tightened. "The Alaskan Sunrise is my property. I'm the only one who can authorize an investigation. Make no mistake about that."

The sheriff gazed at the ceiling, plainly wishing he were someplace else. The detectives looked bored. Slowly, a flush spread across Kendall's face.

Yet, I dismissed all of them the moment I glanced at Corey and saw his reaction. He stood, intent on the men at the foot of the stairs. And the gray eyes were filled with glee.

15

As I followed the family into the living room, I saw Peter stop the sheriff at the front door for a brief conversation, their voices low. He must be asking what to do about his father, I thought, and hoped the sheriff wouldn't be grumpy because he'd made a trip to Meadowmount for nothing.

When Peter finally joined us, I couldn't find a clue in his expression. He sat down beside Gretchen, gave her a faint smile, and held her hand as they sat listening to Corey describe the fire.

He looked tired, slumped in a chair without his usual aura of energy. Once he finished telling us how things had been on the line with the fire crew, he rubbed his eyes and yawned. "They earn their money, those guys," he said. "I thought I was in pretty good shape, but I couldn't keep up with them. I bet they'll be going strong hours from now."

Delphine patted his arm. "Why don't you go upstairs and get some sleep?"

Corey nodded and got slowly to his feet. On his way past, he hooked an arm around my shoulders and kissed the top of my head. I hoped my face didn't reveal the conflicting emotions I felt.

He'd been up half the night helping the fire crew, something that obviously hadn't been easy, even for a jock like Corey. Still, I couldn't forget that curious exultant look in his eyes a few minutes before. And Margaret's comment about Hunter echoed in my mind: "*. . . knew very well who'd poisoned his pet. . . .*"

I watched Corey head toward the hall and saw Hunter standing in the archway, staring at me. He merely jerked his head at Corey as he went by. Then, to my dismay, Hunter came to help Grandpa to his feet and lead him toward the small room off of this one. Delphine always called it, rather grandly, "the library," though I suspected we had a lot more books at home than she had on the few shelves in there.

As it turned out, I didn't have a chance to talk to Grandpa until after lunch. Restless all during the meal, I waited until he pushed his plate back a few inches, his usual signal that he had finished.

"May I help you upstairs, Grandpa?"

Everyone turned to look at me. For a moment,

I thought Delphine was going to protest. Her lips pursed in annoyance, but she said nothing.

"I don't need any help." Grandpa smiled at me. "But I'd welcome your company, Alex."

As I got to my feet, Margaret came from the kitchen and stopped to look at us. Her eyes were red. "Neither of you want dessert?" she asked, sounding disappointed. "It's my own cherry cheesecake. Can't I send some up to you?"

"No, thank you," I murmured.

Grandpa shook his head. "Margaret, girl, my appetite's poor in this heat."

"It's all those peppermints you eat," Delphine said. She sounded exactly like a nasty-nice English nanny, pointing out the shortcomings of her charge.

Gretchen's head came up. "He's almost a hundred years old. He must be doing something right." Her tone wasn't nice at all, merely nasty.

Up in Grandpa's room, the old man eased himself into his chair, put his head back, and sighed. Then he straightened and blinked at me. "I wanted to talk to you, child. I'm glad you made the opportunity. You have something to tell me, don't you?"

I sighed. My face must have betrayed me again. "Yes," I said and leaned forward to hold his hand, frail and cool, in mine.

"At breakfast, Delphine told me she was the one who took the phone from Gretchen's room last Friday. All of us — well, we assumed that trap on the stairs was set for Gretchen. And we thought the way the phone disappeared was part of it, someone making sure she had to go downstairs to answer the phone. It all seemed to fit — until this morning. We hadn't been able to locate the person who called Gretchen, so —"

He peered at me. "And now you've found that person?"

I told him about the call Gretchen received at breakfast. It seemed to come as no surprise to him that there had been such a call on Friday. He was merely interested in the fact that the caller had been identified.

"You're putting the pieces together, aren't you, Alex?"

I nodded slowly.

"Gretchen wasn't the one meant to take that tumble." He closed his eyes and winced. The picture he saw in his mind must have been very painful.

"And you've guessed who the trap was set for — ?" His voice was so low, I had to bend forward to catch the last words.

"Yes," I said. "I think I can guess."

He made a soft sound of regret. "You're a remarkable girl, Alex. Sensible, good head on your shoulders. Something like that — call it maturity — it isn't necessarily a matter of age. What are you, child? Seventeen? Older than I was when I came across the country. We grew up fast then because we had to."

He hesitated and gave me a faint smile. "Guess you've had a taste of that. Your daddy dying — Gretchen says your mama went back to work.

And seems like Corey mentioned you're working, too, saving up for college."

I nodded, but I didn't look at him. He might have been able to read in my eyes how I felt about Corey blabbing something like that. He must have made me sound like Little Orphan Alex.

"Someone like you — even though you're only a slip of a girl — I've talked plain to you. Maybe I've put too much on your shoulders, doing that. The family, we're all too close to this thing. So I've told you things I haven't told the others. Now that may help me, getting it straight in my mind, but — I'm beginning to be afraid that — I've told you too much."

He took his hand from mine and lifted it to touch my cheek. "I even told you the way I've begun to feel about the Sunrise, and that's something I've never breathed to another living soul. An old man rambling, back in the past one minute, and the next. . . . But the way things are going, I'm about convinced that Hunter's been right all along. You should go home. You aren't safe here any longer — not till the trouble's over. If it ever touched you, harmed a hair of your head, I'd never forgive myself."

He looked at me closely. Then he sighed. "I can see it in your face. Something's happened already. Tell me, Alex. I'm an old man, but I've still got a trick or two up my sleeve."

It was a relief, telling all of it at last. Grandpa seemed to know more about what went on than anybody else in the house, anyway. There wasn't a doubt in my mind that he could add it up better, too.

So I told him about the anonymous note that had later been taken from my vanity case, about the slashed photograph left on my pillow, and about the whispered threat on the phone this morning.

"I've been afraid — afraid —" he said, but the old eyes flashed with anger rather than fear. "So you decided to tell me what's been going on."

"Well — I wanted to ask you something, too —"

"What's that?"

I took a deep breath. "Why did Peter's father come to see you?"

He smiled, and all the wrinkles in his face ran in different directions. But somehow his eyes stayed sad. "You're quick, all right," he said, then sobered abruptly as if that worried as well as pleased him.

He smoothed his thin white hair for a moment, and brought his hand down to tap his fingers on the chrome bar of his walker. "I gave Hunter the whole story this morning. If you'll give me your promise to go and pack, let him drive you home this very afternoon, you shall hear it, too."

"I promise."

"Well, then —" He cleared his throat. "Mr. Braun came down to pursue an argument that's been going on for months. There were phone calls, letters — and finally he came in person to settle the thing. What it amounted to was this: the Braun family wants to buy back the shares in their importing firm that my old friend Herman gave me back in 1902."

He paused as a wind-whipped branch lashed at the window. "Herman wanted me to have those shares for my lifetime. But — his family doesn't want my grandson Kendall to control them. From now on, they want the firm to be wholly family-owned.

"I quite understand their feeling. I'd feel the same, under the circumstances. I told Walter Braun that they were more than welcome to my shares. But inasmuch as I hadn't paid a dime for them, I refused to accept any money when the exchange took place. He wouldn't agree to that any more than I'd agree to sell them." He gave me a thin smile. "Two stubborn Germans don't get very far when it comes to settling an argument."

I grinned. There had been a simple explanation, after all, for the mysterious phone calls and letters, one of them special delivery, that had Grandpa in a flap and Gretchen, picking up on it, worried sick.

"Well," Grandpa said, "there may be a way out of the impasse. From the look of things, I'd say a wedding is in the offing, maybe within a year. Gretchen's young, but she's like my Caroline in knowing her mind and heart. Once they're through high school — that'll be in January — let them get married, I say, and go off to college together. And I'll give those shares to them as a wedding gift." His mouth trembled. "I think Walter would be pleased with that solution."

After a moment, he stirred. "Now, Alex, I want you to go find Hunter, even before you pack. Show him that cut-up photograph. Tell him everything we've talked about. Tell him I understand now what's happened. I want him to know that *both* of us know."

"Okay," I said and got to my feet. "I'll tell him. First, I'll get the photograph. He should see that."

I hurried down the hall and opened the door of my room. It was dark and stuffy inside, heavy drapes drawn against the ash-laden air.

Suddenly, something came out of the shadows. A black shape. Strong arms held me, pressing something over my face. Medicine — smelled like medicine — couldn't kick — couldn't bite at that hand holding the damp cloth over my nose and mouth — couldn't even move — too much trouble to try —

I didn't really care anymore by the time the black, humming void closed around me.

16 ▬

When I became conscious again, I thought at first that I was dreaming. In the nightmare, gagged and tied and blindfolded, I lay face down on something that moved and made a lot of noise.

After a few seconds, I realized it was the bed of a truck. I was awake, all right. And hurting, forehead sore, hipbones scraped raw from bouncing on the ridged surface. Scared, too. More than I'd ever been before in my entire life.

I felt a growing outrage, as well. *Why me?* Mingled with all that was a terrible fear about Grandpa's safety. Would this person — someone sick, Hunter said — strike at Grandpa next?

The truck slowed, and I stopped the useless attempt to free myself. It felt as if I'd been tied with my own nylons. And the knots were far too tight for me to hope to get loose.

As the truck came to a stop, men's voices shouted above the clatter of two engines and another dull kind of noise far off in the distance. I could hear only a phrase or two of the brief conversation.

"— you going?"

"— tell the ranger —"

"— road closed ahead —"

Corey's voice! But I had no way of knowing whether he was driving the truck in which I was an unwilling passenger. Or was he in the other vehicle on the road? Had that car come from behind us — or from the opposite direction?

Corey had supposedly headed for bed after being up all night. What errand had been so urgent that he'd left the house again?

Well, whoever the other driver might be, he could help me if I let him know I was tied up in the back of the truck. I lifted my feet, pounded them against the ridged surface beneath me, then slammed my legs hard against the side.

Too late. Both engines accelerated, and the din drowned any noise I'd managed to make. The truck moved again, made a turn. I braced myself as best I could as it bumped and jolted along a rutted side road.

By the time it stopped, I was thoroughly bruised, and in a state of cold, unreasoning terror. Abruptly, I realized what that dull, distant sound meant. We were close enough to hear the roar of the fire!

Someone grabbed my feet, dragged me to the back of the truck. Like a sack of flour, quickly, roughly. Dumped on the ground, my head struck something. It stunned me for a moment.

A door slammed, and the engine roared. Then the sound faded gradually as the truck banged and bumped its way back up that road.

Alone.

Panic jittered through me for several seconds. But when I moaned aloud, the slight sound shamed me, rousing me to anger and then to action.

Dummy! Are you just going to lie here and burn to death?

Rolling over and over on the rough ground, I finally bumped against a rock with edges sharp enough to rub my blindfold off. My heart jolted painfully when I saw an aura of flame outlining the tall pines over the next hill. I lay back panting, paralyzed by fear. It flipped inside my stomach like a crazed wild thing.

After a while, a voice began speaking in my mind, calmly, reasonably. Sometimes the voice was Grandpa's. Sometimes it was Hunter's, sometimes my own.

Easy now. Take it one step at a time. You aren't licked yet. First get rid of the gag. Rub hard against the rock. What if it does scrape your cheek raw? Better scratched than — no, don't think about that. Get a sharp corner under the material and pull till it tears. There.

Even at that moment, the sight of my own pink scarf infuriated me. I shook away the picture of someone pawing through my things for something to tie and gag me. Grimly, I renewed my efforts to saw through the nylon tightly knotted around my wrists.

Something else occupied my mind. From the moment I loosened the blindfold and looked around, I knew where I was, just off the road on the edge of the tree farm. In the other direction, the planted area cut off sharply at the brink of a steep rocky cliff. The moment the fire crossed the road, I would be trapped.

Now I had desperate need of that calming voice in my mind, the words I chanted over and over, first in my head, then aloud in a rasping whisper.

Easy, Alex. One step at a time —

My eyes smarted. I gulped and choked on smoky air, thick with ash, so hot and dry it hurt my lungs. I took short shallow breaths, doggedly sawing at the nylon binding my wrists.

The rough edge of the rock dug into my flesh every time I slipped. I felt little pain, only a vague annoyance. As blood soaked into the material, it made it slippery and my task more difficult.

A burning branch soared overhead, carried on the wind. I watched in helpless horror as it landed in a nearby bush which exploded in flame. Sparks blew around me, igniting the tops of the small trees.

My head filled with a howling noise, either from the fire or the wind that blew my hair across my face, obscuring my vision and further hampering my efforts. With a last desperate lunge at the sharp surface of the rock, I felt the nylon fabric loosen. My hands were free!

In the same moment, with a dull roar, the burning bush sent a stream of fire past the cleared section in front of the first row of trees. Dry brush on both sides of the road blazed up with a high hissing sound.

Almost close enough to touch, a deer leaped past me. As I gasped, something bumped my leg and gave a frightened squeak. For the first time, I became aware of flickers of movement on the ground all around me. Raccoons, possum, rabbits, and chipmunks raced by, an army of forest creatures frantically trying to escape the fire.

As I turned instinctively to follow, I saw a flash of tawny fur and exchanged startled glances with a cougar only a few yards away. We had no interest in each other at that moment. The smaller animals around us paid no attention to the big cat, either, as they ran from a greater danger.

I registered the details of the scene automatically. This must be the mate of the cat Niles said the dogs had killed. No matter. The animals were luckier than I. They could make a run for safety, ahead of the fire. Hobbled, I couldn't.

Crawling toward the stream, I realized the road was now cut off. I suppose I sought a place to delay the inevitable, inching along the rough ground toward water with the instinct of any hurt, dazed animal.

At the sound of an engine, my head came up and a hammerblow of fear cut off my breath. The truck had come back! It appeared through smoke and orange tongues of flame, an old red pickup

Niles used to drive around the ranch. But he wasn't driving it now. Relief swept over me as I saw Hunter at the wheel.

A huge half-dead pine by the side of the road burst into flame spontaneously from its thick trunk to the top spreading limbs. Hunter braked the truck, leaped out, and ran to kneel by my side.

He'd arrived like an avenging angel, his face dark with anger. "What have they done to you?"

"I'm okay," I insisted when I could get my voice to work. Actually, I was far beyond the point where I could feel bruises and scrapes and bumps and cuts, or even minor burns. But the blessed numbness of physical hurts didn't ease my emotional agony.

"Grandpa! Is Grandpa all right? I've been so worried —"

"Got to get you out of here." Hunter didn't bother to free my ankles. He scooped me up and turned toward the truck.

An enormous flaming limb crashed down on the cab, then another across the hood. In the seconds that Hunter stood, frozen, the truck was enveloped.

"Let's get to the water!"

In a stumbling run, he carried me to the point where the stream was deepest. Perhaps two feet of water had collected there in a small pool beneath the rocks. Above, the waterfall spilled down from the outlet to the underground spring. A grassy embankment on the other side offered some protection from the direct, blast-furnace heat of the oncoming inferno.

Awkwardly, Hunter rolled me into the pool. That cold water felt marvelous, even though I instantly recovered sensation in each burn and abrasion. I ducked my face again and again until my hair hung in dripping strands around my face.

My mind seemed to revive along with my parched body. I realized that Hunter was trying to free my ankles. The knots were even tighter now that they were wet, so at last he pulled off my sandals and dragged the twisted strands of nylon down over my feet. Then he lay down in the water beside me.

"Grandpa — you didn't answer me — is Grandpa all right?"

Hunter spoke close to my ear. "He's fine. Sent me to look for you. He wanted to get a message to the ranger in charge down here — and then he found out you never talked to me — and we discovered you were gone."

"But Corey — what was Corey doing on the road? I thought he was sleeping —"

"I woke him up, sent him on ahead with the message. Couldn't leave Grandpa until I rounded up Peter to stand guard — and Pete was on the grounds helping the men with the stock. When Corey got back and told me he met Niles's truck on the way —" His face twisted with frustration. "If I'd got to you one minute sooner —"

"I'm glad Grandpa's safe, anyway." I bent to wet my burning face again.

"They won't hurt him," Hunter said, his voice harsh. "Everybody's sitting around in his bedroom watching one another, scared silly — though it's a little late for that — even though they don't know what's going on."

"They haven't guessed?"

He poured water over my head from his cupped hand. "Aside from Grandpa, I doubt it. Maybe Corey's finally figured out part of it. That message to the ranger said to look for a car and body in the burned area."

He shook his head, dark hair plastered across his forehead. "I still can't make sense of it. If they thought you had the Sunrise and searched your room and didn't find it — why did they try to —?"

"You mean they *don't* have the Sunrise?"

"Grandpa says they don't."

I didn't puzzle over that at the time, because something fell into the stream with a loud hiss only a few feet from us. I felt a sudden surge of heat and ducked back into the water. Hunter got on his knees, trying to shield me with his body. That made him vulnerable to the firebrands that came hurtling on the wind to fall around us. One of them burned him across the shoulder before I pulled him down beside me.

"You're the bravest girl I've ever known." He leaned over to kiss me, and he must have realized then that I wasn't so brave, because even my lips were trembling. "We'll come through okay, Alex. We have to — so I'll have a chance to tell you — how I feel about you. I didn't even know what was happening to me. Never felt this way before. And then — when I found out you'd disappeared — just like Peter's father — it hit me. I couldn't stand it if anything happened to you." He ended fiercely, with his arms around me, "We'll be all right. We're in a good spot. You'll see. Don't be scared. It'll be rough for a while, but — we'll make it."

I wasn't all that sure. I couldn't even be sure he meant what he said. At a moment like that, he'd just want to keep my spirits up, to comfort me in any way he could.

"I'm sorry you got in this mess trying to rescue me," I said, "but I'm awfully glad I don't have to go through this — all alone."

The booming noise of the fire came closer with occasional loud cracks, like gunfire. I could hear Hunter's ragged breathing in my ear, feel the rapid beat of his heart. After those first few fearful moments, my panic gradually subsided.

I lost track of time then, lost all awareness except of the noise around us and the almost unbearable heat. Fiery pitch-filled pinecones arced through the air like shooting stars. Above us, towering flames soared toward the night sky until it seemed as if we were watching from the bottom of a pit in hell.

Hunter ripped two pieces of cloth from his shirt, and we held them over our faces, ducking beneath the water again and again. Finally, we lay with only our mouths and noses above the surface.

Now, burning debris showered down on us,

one branch blistering Hunter's arm before he managed to push it away. My hands and neck were seared by another. I saw several long strands of my hair floating away, tangled around a smoking twig.

An eternity later, the noise faded. Warily, I lifted my head to listen. I didn't hear the sudden *whoosh!* that signaled a new outbreak of fire, with a resultant blast of heat on my face. I wondered if I were imagining that the wind had died down, too.

The little trees were gone. Nothing but smouldering trunks remained, flashing a deep orange in every current of air. Beyond, the tall pines were still pillars of bright yellow flame against the dark sky. All we could see were smoking stumps, blackened rock, and the burning trees.

"It's over," I said, my voice so hoarse I hardly recognized it. "Thank God. It's gone past us."

17

S lowly, we sat up. But when I tried to stand Hunter held me back. "We can't walk out," he said. "My foot's blistered, and your sandals are gone. We'd have third degree burns before we were halfway to the road. We'll have to wait for the fire crew."

I settled back beside him. "Hunter, did you *really* think we'd make it?"

He grinned at me, his teeth startlingly white in his flushed, streaked face. "I was pretty sure you would," he said. "And I figured I'd probably get through okay, too — if only to give you hell for almost getting yourself killed. Why didn't you go home when I told you to?"

I was too exhausted to work up the faintest spark of anger. "You never asked me in the right way." I thought, *Later I'll realize that's a crazy thing to say. Maybe tomorrow, I'll laugh.*

175

Hunter put his arms around me. "If I'd said, 'Alex, you're very special to me. I don't want anything to happen to you. I want you to be where you're safe' — would you have paid any attention then?"

"Probably not," I said, resting my head against his shoulder, "but that would have been the right way to ask."

He laughed.

"Hunter," I said, my eyes so heavy I couldn't keep them open any longer, "you can take it all back if you want. I mean, all those things you said — when you couldn't be sure we'd — we'd come out of this alive. I know it was just — you knew how scared I was —"

"You think I wasn't scared? You think I was only trying to keep you from falling apart? You think I didn't mean every word? Listen, from the very first minute I picked you up at your house, I haven't been tracking. You'd turned into the most sensationally pretty girl I've ever seen. Not only that —"

"That's nice," I murmured. And fell asleep while he was still talking.

He said later that he'd dozed for a while, too. When I finally woke up, he was patting my face gently, water in his cupped palm.

"The prettiest girl," he said, and his voice was ragged. "Your eyebrows are singed, your cheek's scraped raw, and there's a lump on your forehead the size of a walnut. You've lost some hunks of hair, too. I think you're going to have to settle for a crewcut. Don't worry. You'll still be the most beautiful girl in the state, possibly on the whole West Coast."

This time I managed a shaky laugh. "If you only knew — I fell in love with you years ago, the first time I saw you. And you never looked at me twice."

"You were — what? Fourteen? In braids — braces on your teeth." Hunter grinned. "Come on, gimme a break. How was I supposed to know you'd turn out like this?"

He kissed me, very gently but for a long time.

"You've been acting rotten," I said. "Ever since the first day. How come you were so good at hiding what you said you were thinking about me? Talk about mean —"

"Yeah," he said. "Guess I was at that. Well, I went into shock — but it was more than — just reacting to the way you look." He hesitated. "I didn't know that until — until Grandpa lit into me."

"Grandpa did? When?"

"Well, I went down and banged on your door, and then poked my head in. And saw you were gone. Suitcase wasn't packed, and I caught a whiff of something. The room was stuffy, all closed up. Didn't tell Grandpa — he was frantic enough — but I thought it might be chloroform." He squeezed my hand.

"Anyway, I went tearing back to tell him you were gone, raving like a maniac about — well, about how I kept at you to go home and you wouldn't — and now something had happened — and if you'd had the sense God gave a gnat — well, you get the idea."

I gave a short laugh. I got the picture, all right. It would have saved a lot of wear and tear on my disposition a couple days ago if I'd realized then that Hunter only lost his temper when he was worried about someone. Someone special to him.

"Grandpa really laid me out. He said we should have protected you better, and that was a mistake, all right. But the only mistake you'd made was in caring about us — about him and Gretchen and me. So much that you tried to help, I mean, and that's what landed you in trouble. And I'd better stop judging people and start helping, too, or he'd have my hide." A sheepish smile.

"He's always tried to teach us about money, that there's a lot of responsibility connected with it, but pleasure, too. And what he means by that is, it's really great being able to help people. The way Gretchen and I learned that over the years was by watching him, the kick he gets out of giving his money away. Because he loves people, loves being able to help."

"Yes," I said. "That's why everybody's so crazy about him."

Hunter looked at me, his dark eyes serious. "I think you should know — he'd decided long before any of this heavy stuff happened that he wanted to put you through college."

"Me? College?" I stared at him. "What a wonderful old man. I — I can hardly believe it."

We were both silent for a while. I guess we were thinking the same thing. Grandpa would be climbing the walls by now. I wished there were some way to let him know we were all right.

"I keep going back to what you said about not protecting me," I said at last. "You did tell me not to trust anybody at Meadowmount. Especially Corey." I looked at him. "Margaret told me the rest of the story about Rufus. That you — that you found him."

Hunter nodded. "Funny. After all these years — I said something to Corey. Telling you about it kind of stirred it all up again. I told him straight out, I figured he was the one who poisoned Rufus."

I drew in my breath. "What did he say?"

"He can't ever come right out and admit anything. He always takes a step past something like that. So he just shrugged as if he were saying, 'Well, what can I do about it now?' And then he said he'd been trying to make it up to me ever since."

I sighed. I had a lot to learn when it came to judging character.

"So I said, 'By making a play for Alex? That's how you're making it up to me?' And then he accused me of being jealous." Hunter looked thoughtful. "Guess he made me wonder about us. And then I knew — I cared about you, too."

"I'm glad," I said. "Hunter, we've got a lot of catching up to do. Let's not talk about anybody but us right now. Until we have to go back and —"

He kissed me again. I guess we talked for an hour or more until we heard the roar of a truck. It came bumping in to brake sharply behind the burned-out frame of Niles's red pickup.

We must have been a weird sight to see when we limped through the front door at Meadowmount, arms around each other's shoulders, our clothes torn and filthy and sopping wet.

Delphine came from the living room to meet us, her face reflecting her struggle with conflicting emotions, horror at our condition — and concern about the carpeting in the hall. At the same time, obviously, she seemed to be groping for the right thing to say to two people who have narrowly escaped death.

"Hunter! Alex! Are you — how on earth did you get so — so wet?"

Peter and Gretchen were only a step behind her. As Peter gripped Hunter's hand, his eyes shining, Gretchen burst into tears.

"You're both safe!" she gulped. "Oh, Alex, if anything had happened to you, it would have been all — all my fault." Her eyes widened. "Oh, but you're *hurt!* Come to the kitchen. Margaret's a whiz at first aid. Why — what's the matter?"

She had seen me stiffen, my head jerking back involuntarily as she said the housekeeper's name in a warm, natural voice. During the worst hours and in all the waiting time since the danger passed, neither Hunter or I had mentioned the name of the person who brought terror to Meadowmount.

From the top of the stairs, Corey said into the

brief silence, "When it comes to first aid, I'm your man, Gretch. Something tells me both these people would rather take their chances with me. Isn't that right?"

Down in the hall, when he'd had a closer look at us, his mouth tightened. He gestured toward the library. "In there, you two. Delphine, how about getting some hot water and soft rags? And disinfectant. And bandages and burn ointment. Gretch, you and Peter can rustle up some dry clothes. Pajamas, maybe? Something loose fitting and cool —"

"And please tell Grandpa we're all right," I said as she looked both reluctant to leave and eager to help.

Delphine sniffed. "He's been asleep for hours."

"Want to bet?" Gretchen settled herself in the chair elevator, Peter already loping up the stairs ahead of her.

An hour later, we assembled in Grandpa's room. He sat in his big chair, a small figure in absurd red-and-white striped pajamas, white hair neat as if he had just brushed it. His eyes looked tired, but his smile was wide and warm as he held out his hands to us.

"Thank God," he murmured as I kissed his cheek. "Thank God. I guess we all made some bad mistakes." He looked from my face to Hunter's and back again, then at our clasped hands. "And maybe we corrected one or two," he observed with satisfaction.

From his seat in the corner, Kendall said impatiently, "Could we get on with it, Grandpa? I think the best thing for Hunter and Alex would be a good night's sleep. What's left of the night, anyway. They're in bad shape, both of them. Can't we leave the questions and answers till morning?"

"No," the old man said wearily. "The sheriff or one of the rangers will be knocking at the door before dawn, anyway. I gave Niles instructions to leave the gate open."

"The sheriff?" Kendall scowled. There was still an edge to his voice.

"After tonight, there'll be a new investigation. Corey?" Grandpa turned to him, seated beside Gretchen and Peter on the bed. "You'd better explain about the message you took to the rangers this afternoon."

Corey straightened and rubbed his eyes. His expression was bleak. "I asked them to look for a car — and a body — in the burned area, the section that was first to go. A small compact car —"

"Mr. Braun drove —" The words burst from Delphine. She caught herself, glanced at Peter, then back at Corey. "Is that who —?"

He nodded. "They found him," he said in a controlled voice. "The call came through an hour ago."

"But what —? He said he might be called away suddenly — at almost any time," Delphine said in a curious piping voice. "He said that. Margaret heard him —"

"And took advantage of that fact," Grandpa interrupted. "Because she also overheard something else. Mr. Braun told me, if he found the *fluchthelfer* wasn't on the up and up, he'd try to get him jailed for fraud. He'd do that the moment he reached home. Well, he was expecting a call from some people up in San Francisco — they publish a German newspaper, so they have contacts all over Europe. All I can surmise is — that call came through late Friday night —"

"Yes," I said. "I heard the phone ring — late —"

"And Margaret may have listened on the kitchen phone — not the first time that's happened." He sighed. "She chose to believe — what she wanted to believe — what she had to believe at that point. That her informant was telling the truth. And she'd see her sister again — if Mr. Braun could be — silenced."

He turned to Peter. The sadness on his face made him look a thousand years old. "My heart shares your loss," he said softly. "Your family's grief is my grief."

Peter nodded slowly.

Studying him, I realized that he had been braced for trouble, even tragedy, since the night of my arrival. He had not known until the following morning, however, what form it might take.

"Oh, Peter!" Gretchen sounded close to tears once more. Then she whirled toward her grandfather. "But how can you be sure that — are you saying that *Margaret* — that she's been doing all these awful things?"

Grandpa glanced at me, a plea in his eyes. I went to sit by Gretchen and took her hand. "I know how much it must hurt to hear that, Gretch. Alden helped, naturally. He's always gone along with anything she wanted."

I remembered the hoarse whisper on the phone that morning. *"You could get hurt, playing games like this —"* Alden, of course. It would take me a while to forget what he'd done.

"Margaret must have been — sick — for quite a while. Can you imagine the strain — trying to make the decision about ransoming her sister? And then you fell downstairs — and that trap had been meant for Peter's father —"

"Oh, *no*." Gretchen groped blindly, and Peter shoved a handkerchief in her hand. "It's like — the whole world's gone crazy. First, Bonnie turns out to be the rat of all time —"

"What?" I said, bewildered.

"I didn't tell you the truth — there was so much going on this morning." Gretchen straightened, took a deep steadying breath. "She let something drop and I nailed her. She was the one who sent you that anonymous letter. So you were right all the time. You never did like her."

Win a few, lose a few, I thought wearily. Well, Corey might have been a monster as a little kid, but there was a chance he meant what he'd said to Hunter. Maybe he was trying to make up for it.

I had a hunch the glee I'd seen in his eyes that morning had reflected nothing more sinister than amusement over Grandpa's five-star general behavior.

Remembering how gentle he'd been, tending to

our burns and bruises, I could forgive a lot. Perhaps Hunter would, too, eventually.

But Bonnie — I suspected she'd been the one who slashed my picture. Perhaps with Hunter's help, I could smuggle another copy into Gretchen's room so she'd never have to know what happened to the original. She had enough to cope with right then, accepting the fact that Margaret had been responsible for the death of Peter's father.

"Grandpa," she said now, "how did you find out?"

"I couldn't be sure at first. I only suspected what might have happened . . ."

As his voice drifted off, I glanced at the picture covering the dumbwaiter shaft. I couldn't have said when I first realized the true significance of the moment in this room when we heard the voices from the kitchen. At some point, however, I became aware of the fact that voices from this room could be heard just as clearly in the room below.

Grandpa heard about things going on in the household, listening to Margaret discuss them in the kitchen.

And Margaret had listened to him. I recalled the things she'd muttered about the Sunrise and idols of gold. And then she said, "Even Mr. Luther says there's a curse on it."

Yet, Grandpa claimed he'd never told another living soul how he had come to feel about the Sunrise.

When Margaret overheard our last discussion, something must have snapped in her mind, already under too much stress. Maybe she decided to get rid of me as another threat to her plans — or perhaps she was still convinced that I had stolen the Sunrise, and this might be her last chance to get her hands on it. Had she really been foolish enough to think she could sell it — or hold it for ransom — to get the money to buy her sister's freedom?

What *had* happened to the Sunrise? When I asked Hunter if 'they' — and we both knew that meant Margaret and Alden — had the Sunrise, he had told me, "Grandpa says they don't."

I looked at the old man quickly and saw a flicker of amusement in his eyes, as if he'd been following my thoughts. Casually, he patted the pocket of his big chair. *The old rascal!* I thought, and grinned at him. He must have overheard enough to make him suspect an attempt would be made to steal the Sunrise. So the necklace had conveniently "disappeared."

Kendall spoke jerkily as if he were just emerging from shock. "Margaret! And Alden, too. Why, they're almost like family. I had no idea she took that swindler seriously, that ridiculous story about her sister." His eyes glazed as he turned to me. "But why — why did they try to — to do away with you, Alex?"

Hunter said shortly, "They were sure she had the Sunrise, for one thing. If you'll think back, Dad, the way you acted, they must have figured that's what you thought, too. Besides, Alex was getting too close to the truth."

We all started at the sound of a car racing down the drive, tires squealing.

Kendall struggled to his feet. "But that must be — they're getting away!"

As he hurried from the room followed by Delphine, Grandpa beckoned to me. He said softly when I bent over him, "You might close it now. The panel over the dumbwaiter."

I did as he asked.

"Peter and I agreed to leave the panel open," he said with a glance at the couple on the couch, their arms around each other. "We figured Margaret and Alden would listen in the kitchen, that they'd try to make a run for it.

"It's best if the end of the story doesn't happen here at Meadowmount. Too hard on Gretchen, seeing Margaret taken into custody. Too hard on all of us." He made a soft sound. "There's a roadblock into the fire area. And word has gone out — they won't be allowed to pass."

I took his hand and brought it to my cheek.

"So — we can all get back to our beds now." He raised his voice slightly as Kendall reappeared in the door. "You were right, we need our rest. Let the other questions and answers wait till morning."

He lifted a wrinkled hand to remove his glasses, and Luther von Weber went off the air.